To Dad and Becky. Without you this book would be much worse. X

Dear reader,

You are loved. Even if you don't know it yet, you are loved. Even if you don't understand what that fully means. You are loved. You wouldn't be here on Earth, reading this book, if that wasn't true. You are loved.

The Fairy Tale

Part One

Prologue

"Dad! Don't go up there," Maye called, flying onto the roof of the dining hall.

The latest arrow to hit Axone's wing had caused the most damage so far and, in a panic, Maye had flown to help him. But she was nine months pregnant and couldn't do much more.

The fear that laced his daughter's words penetrated Axone with the sharpness of another arrow. He shook it off. This war between The Kingdom and Lorkun Lodge needed to be won and, finally, his army were winning it. He flew to the top of a flagpole which had been erected in the courtyard to mark the college's 50th anniversary. The humans who were celebrating and feasting inside the dining hall had no idea there was a war being fought outside among the fairies, with one side fighting to protect them.

Maye crouched down on the roof, using her hands to support her stomach. A deep aching pain started behind her eyes then began pressing at her temples while she watched her dad on top of the flagpole. She saw him slip slightly before quickly regaining his balance. The wobble was uncharacteristic and noticing it sent a jolt of tension through Maye's body. The injured wing was having more effect on Axone's ability to fight than he would admit.

Axone regained his balance on the pole and reached behind him for another arrow, keeping his eyes focused on the target. He positioned the arrow in the bow and pulled back the string until it was so taut it nearly snapped. He aimed it with a precision that could only be reached through years of meticulous practice.

Axone steadied his arm. Once Vantar was defeated, this war would be won. Lorkun Lodge would no longer have their powerful leader. He checked one last time that the angle was exact. It was.

"Dad!"

Three Lorkun fairies dived down onto Axone before he could fire the arrow. He slipped under their weight and fell from the pole, banging his head on the mast before falling and hitting the concrete below with a solid thud and a loud crack. He lay there, unmoving.

Maye flew down to the spot where he landed, arriving just after he made his first attempt to move. She saw the fierce pain flash through his eyes before he had time to compose himself.

"Dad," she said, as she lowered her body onto the ground next to him.

She put one arm beneath his back, the other beneath the bend in his knees, and carried him into a dark corner of the foyer, by the large double doors that opened into the bustling dining hall.

The news had spread quickly outside that Axone, godfather of The Kingdom, had been successfully taken down and when they saw Maye carrying his limp body inside, Vantar had cheered. The Lorkun fairies flew off behind Vantar back to the Lodge knowing that, while the war was not yet over, an important battle had just been won.

Maye sat down by Axone's body on the dark grey floor, the bump of her unborn son filling the gap between them, and gently uncrumpled her dad's wings. She reminded herself to breathe steadily, so as not to distress the baby.

She took a deep breath and put one hand on her father's forehead.

"You're okay, Dad. They've gone away. You don't need to fight anymore."

Axone opened his eyes and looked at his daughter.

"Maye," he said. "Remember. Whatever happens, the humans are always worth fighting for."

Maye looked down. She often struggled to believe this, and she struggled now more than ever.

"They don't even know we do it," said Maye.

She moved her arm behind his head to try and provide more support.

"Are you in pain, Dad?" she asked.

"Maye, honey, I've been down here on Earth too long," he said.

"Don't worry, we're going back up," said Maye, but in the same moment she felt her dad's head become heavier in her arm.

"A fairy can't survive down here too long with a damaged wing," he said quietly.

"Yes, let's go. We'll just quickly head back up."

"It's too far. I won't make it. Going through the atmosphere to The Kingdom is too much strain. I won't make it, sweetie."

"Fairies can't die," said Maye, her eyes beginning to glisten with tears. "You know that, Dad." She was talking to herself now. Axone's eyes had just closed. "Fairies can't die," she said again.

But they both knew fairies could die. If the unthinkable act was committed of one immortal piercing another immortal with an arrow while on Earth, a fairy could die.

Maye's statement hung in the air, her words slowly evaporating into the silence of the foyer, past the double doors behind which the lively dinner celebrations continued.

Axone's now subtle movements, in which Maye was pinning all her hope, became gradually smaller until the gentle rise and fall of his chest slowed to a halt. Maye bowed her head onto her dad's chest. He was still lying in her arms, but he was no longer there. Maye closed her eyes. Her tightly shut lids held back almost all the tears.

Chapter One

Seventeen years later…

Axone Junior stretched his arms up into the hot summer air then lay back on the roof of the car, a gentle breeze cooling his smooth, seventeen-year-old skin. The metal beneath him had warmed up under the strong afternoon sun and, as he closed his eyes, a droplet of sweat ran down the side of his head into his silk, chocolate hair.

Axone Junior was an undeniably good-looking fairy. His perfectly positioned features and glimmering green eyes were inherited from his grandfather; the grandfather who died just two days before his grandson was born.

He was just about to doze off while waiting for the human who owned the car to pay for their petrol, when a loud crash sent him bolt upright and flying into the air. A second crash followed the first, and the human came running through the station's automatic doors holding magazines, crisps, and a selection of fizzy canned drinks in her arms.

"Oh no," he thought. "I might have picked the wrong human to hitch a ride with today."

Next a male, wearing a padded black jacket and waving a walkie-talkie in his hand, burst through the doors running and shouting after her.

Axone Junior flew back down and held on tight to the car's aerial as the lady jumped in the driver's seat, threw the stolen items in the back, turned the key in the ignition, and sped off before the security guard came close.

They were travelling fast down the motorway now and Axone Junior's arms were feeling weak holding onto the aerial at this speed. He needed to get off and hitch a ride with someone else, but he was not strong enough to fly anywhere on his own right now. He needed to get back up to The Kingdom to recharge his wings before he could do that. He would just have to keep holding on as tight as he could. Falling onto a motorway would be fatal for a fairy who, like Axone Junior, had a deformed wing. He would be crushed within seconds if he fell.

The car made a sudden stop and, before he could get a better grip, the vehicle had spun around so fast that it flung him from the roof and into the air.

"Woah!" he called as he whizzed up into the empty space above the motorway.

He looked at the car beneath him which was now tumbling down the side of the grassy bank, flipping and crashing. He felt a strong jerk on his neck, and suddenly he could only see sky. A robin had him in his beak.

Axone Junior relaxed into the strength of the bird's mouth. They flew to a nearby electricity pylon and found their balance on the metal pole. Fairies and robins were roughly the same size when they stood up straight. Axone Junior stared at the motorway below, while cars zoomed past in a blur.

"What were you doing out there?" asked the robin, smoothing out his ruffled breast feathers.

"I thought I was just going for a casual ride," Axone Junior replied avoiding eye contact while slightly shuffling his feet. "I don't have my own humans, so I pick different ones to look out for and to hitch a ride with. I think I made a mistake this time."

The robin didn't respond but looked at Axone Junior, then tilted his head. "Axone Junior?" he asked.

Axone Junior turned to look at him.

"You're Axone's grandson, aren't you?" the robin asked.

Axone Junior's grandfather was the first fairy to have been so loved and respected that he was known beyond The Kingdom of the fairies and was celebrated among the birds of the sky, too. His fame extended to his grandson.

"You almost died," the robin continued. "And, if you are Axone's grandson, I thought you were not supposed to be alone on Earth?"

Axone Junior ignored the comment, frustrated at its truth.

"I need to get back up to The Kingdom as quickly as possible," Axone Junior said. "If you can get me two miles up my right wing will be strong enough to do the rest. Also, please call me Ax."

"Okay, Ax," said the robin.

The robin flew up as far as he could manage with Ax in his beak, which, happily, was a little more than the two miles Ax required. The beginning of the fairy atmosphere was sixty-two miles above Earth, but the effort it took to fly lessened the further you were from Earth's surface, and Ax reckoned that two miles would be enough this time.

"Thank you," said Ax when the robin let go. "Please don't tell anyone about this."

"Don't worry, I won't. And Axone's grandson?" the robin smiled. "They wouldn't believe me anyway."

The robin flew back down and Ax pushed, in pain, to complete the last bit of the journey, flying much slower than the typical fairy speed, and the strain on his body was immense.

He crashed through The Kingdom's front door into the grand open lobby, collapsed onto the terracotta tiles by the entrance, and caught his breath. He could hear delicate chatter in the corridors around him, but, thankfully, the lobby was momentarily empty. He rearranged the sleeves of his black t-shirt, ran his hands through his smooth hair, then wiped the sweat from his face. He leant forward and looked at his reflection in the silver plant pot next to him. He looked nearly normal.

Ax rested his head against the wooden wall behind him, closed his eyes, and thought about how close he had just come to death. Again.

He couldn't help it. He had to keep going down to Earth. The desire was deep in the cells of his blood. The desire was deep in all fairies' blood. All fairies were born to help humans, but Ax's damaged wing made it difficult for him to travel between The Kingdom and Earth.

His broken wing also meant he was not given responsibility for specific humans the way other fairies were, and he frequently weighed up the pros and cons of this. One pro was that he had the freedom to be obsessed with all humans and, as a result, while feeling no particular loyalty, he could see the beauty and joy in all of them. Even the ones who robbed a petrol station, got chased by security, then crashed down a grassy bank. On the other hand, fairies frequently talked about why their allotted human was incredible, and Ax was excluded from these discussions. As fairies in The Kingdom grew older, they were often given more humans to watch out for, and some cared for as many as seven hundred humans.

There were, however, two humans to whom Ax had particularly warmed, and it had been them he had wanted to see today, before his dodgy ride to their school waylaid him. The two humans he liked were called Harper and Jesse.

They shared the same A-Level maths class at Marlborough High School in England, but they shared little else. Harper was an introvert. Jesse was an extrovert. Harper was a loner. Jesse was popular. In fact, the only other thing they had in common besides A-Level maths was that Ax had just nearly died trying to see them both.

He had to be more careful.

If his mum found out, she would be disappointed. Maye seldom placed rules on Ax but he had known, for as long as he could remember, that there were restrictions on him that the other fairies did not have. He knew his broken wing meant that, unlike other fairies, he was not immortal.

***

A bell rang throughout The Kingdom, and Ax jumped up off the floor. His energy was sufficiently recharged, and the echoing chimes signalled it was time to eat.

He rolled his shoulders back, stretched out his neck, plastered on a smile, and headed towards the dining hall. He turned left down the first corridor, flying over the soft, golden carpets which lay between the oak-panelled walls and wondered how many secrets were tangled between the golden threads shining below him. He flew beneath the shimmering chandeliers, flicking his eyes up towards the white bulbs that glistened amongst the intricate metallic designs. The light fixtures were switched on all the time because light and dark (and therefore day and night) did not exist in The Kingdom the way they did on Earth.

Ax remembered the lessons he attended in fairy school about day and night and how these two states governed human life on Earth. The young fairies had been taught that every twenty-four hours day was replaced by night to remind humans that they were not in control. They were also taught about a special time called dawn, when night merged with day, which was a time of promise and renewal for humans and was a thrilling time to be awake. They had been taught that night provided two different experiences for humans depending on their needs. It could be a time of restoration and repair, achieved through a process called sleep. Or it could be a time of wrestling with dark thoughts and painful feelings of fear and suffering. For those in the second group, fears would begin to disappear as the sun rose during dawn. Thoughts would slow back down, and coffee would be drunk. Lessons learnt would sometimes stay, and sometimes leave to be relearnt another time.

Ax remembered the fairy teacher explaining that whatever the humans experienced during night, all of them changed in some way every twenty-four hours.

Ax smiled fondly to himself at the memory of those lessons. He continued towards the dining hall, smells of fresh, warm bread rolls now hitting his nostrils, and flew past the out-of-bounds room which glowed a continuous gold and was the only room in the whole of The Kingdom that was not accessible to the fairies. Only Maye and her three carefully chosen Elders – Elba, Elrin and Elson – were allowed in the out-of-bounds room. Maye, Elba, Elrin and Elson had their governance meetings in there. But no one, not even Ax, knew exactly what went on behind the perpetual golden glow.

Naturally, rumours bounced around The Kingdom about why it was out-of-bounds, but the truth was that no-one was certain of what went on behind those doors. Ax had, however, been in there once. He couldn't remember it in any detail (he was merely hours old), and Maye always deflected questions about it. But he had been taken in there in the first moments following his birth. Ax sometimes had vague flashbacks of being bathed in a golden light, but any more detail eluded him.

As Ax entered the lavish dining hall he thought, once again, about what exactly might be in the out-of-bounds room, and about what had happened to him in there seventeen years earlier.

He flew to the first empty seat and sat down in front of a bowl of hot vegetable soup with a bread roll and a large wedge of salty yellow butter on the side. It was a phenomenal combination of Earth food.

Fairies had the ability to replicate any Earth food or drink that they desired. It looked, smelt, and tasted exactly as the original. Ax's knife clinked gently against the cream china as he picked up a generous slab of butter from the side dish and began spreading it onto the roll.

Chapter Two

"Finish your soup or you're not getting up from the table," the dinner lady said to Jesse in her no-nonsense tone, wiping bits of food off the table next to them with a dripping wet cloth.

It was Monday lunchtime at Marlborough High School on Earth and most of the kids had finished their lunch, but Jesse had started late.

Jesse was a relaxed human whose dark curls lolled on top of his head in the same chilled manner with which his limbs moved around his body. He had the kind of good hair and skin that can only be achieved through good genes, and that no number of expensive products or video tutorials would allow you to mimic. He was popular and knew how to look someone up and down just long enough for them to wish for that kind of attention again one day.

"This is bullshit," Jesse spluttered to his friend Mark, who was sitting next to him and had already finished eating.

"Yeah, well, there are people who get hardly any food at all in other countries," said Mark, raising both eyebrows as he looked at Jesse.

"There are people in other countries who would refuse to eat this," said Jesse. "I mean, this is not even a vegetable" – he picked a soggy beige square from the broth and watched the bottom half fall back in with a plop – "it's against my principles to eat something that could be twelve different things and even after swallowing it I still can't tell what it is." He let go of the bit of vegetable that remained in his fingers and watched it drop back into the soup.

"It's good for you," said Mark who never had such a problem with the food as Jesse did.

"Dancing all night is good for me," said Jesse as he poured the remaining soup onto the table just as the dinner lady turned her back.

The boys stood up to leave and the soup started dripping off the grey plastic table onto the matching grey floor.

"Bye!" Jesse called into the kitchen with a grin, picking up a muffin on the way out, and leaving his now empty bowl on the table. "I don't know why they think they get to treat us like kids here," Jesse continued as they walked down the noisy school corridor and out toward the playground to join a game of football. "They think they're our parents. But not even my parents would make me eat that shit."

"They are legally our guardians while we're in school," said Mark. "I don't know why you refuse to eat the healthy food just because it looks weird, then happily drench your organs in alcohol on the weekends."

"That's good for the soul," said Jesse, putting one hand on Mark's shoulder and breaking into a grin with all his teeth on show. "The booze, the socialising, the girls. They're all good for the soul. Being force fed boiled vegetables? That's good for nothing. That is what will make me sick." He took his hand off Mark's shoulder. "That is what will put me in a bad mood and being in a bad mood makes you sick."

"Whatever," said Mark who was used to Jesse's over-the-top speeches.

"If you are chilled and happy you could eat dog biscuits for every meal of your life and you would outlive someone who drinks kale smoothies but is a miserable sod," Jesse added.

The two boys dropped their bags by the make-shift goal posts and ran onto the football pitch under the warm, September sun.

**

Jesse and Harper queued up alongside each other outside Miss Grinter's maths class.

"Come on in," Miss Grinter called, one hand holding the door open, the other hand holding a coffee and motioning them in while trying not to spill it.

The students walked in past her upright posture and brown skirt-suit, the familiar smell of too much perfume trying to hide the odour of coffee.

"Shirt. Shirt. Shirt," Miss Grinter barked at almost every student as they walked in, including Jesse.

Miss Grinter noticed an untucked shirt before she noticed the child inside it.

Of course, it did not actually matter whether a shirt was tucked in or not, but creating the rule gave the school a chance to establish some authority on an issue that did not really affect anyone. At the same time, it gave the students a chance to push back harmlessly at that authority in an attempt to regain a little control. Teenagers who needed the most control, often due to a lack of it in their homelife, would, when challenged on an untucked shirt, subtly fold it up instead. Or, they would untuck it again as soon as they were sat at their desk, confirming, to themselves, that they still had a little power remaining.

The students shuffled into their assigned seats and Jesse untucked his shirt as soon as he sat down at his desk. He sat in the middle row of the maths class, as he always did, with a bag that was empty, as it always was, and so started the lesson in need of a pen, as he always did.

Harper sat at the back of the class, as she always did. Her equipment was laid out carefully in front of her, as it always was, and her handwriting fell neatly on the lines, as it always did. Harper kept to herself as much as possible and her detachment from the social world was puzzling to the other students, when indeed they ever noticed her, which was rare.

Miss Grinter pulled the lid off her black marker and wrote 'The Golden Ratio' across the top of the whiteboard, then underlined it and added the date on the right.

"So, what do we already know about the golden ratio?" Miss Grinter asked, putting the lid back on the pen and turning around to face the class.

The low-level chatter dissipated, and the ensuing silence told the teacher she would be starting from scratch.

"The golden ratio," Miss Grinter began to explain, now perching on the corner of her desk, "is used to determine whether something will look pleasing or not. It is a mathematical formula that can determine whether we will consider an object, or animal, or person – regardless of culture or personal taste – as beautiful. As you will already know, it's our Headmaster's favourite topic and he insists new A-Level maths students study it every year."

There was a murmuring. Then Harper, who rarely spoke in class, put up her hand.

"Yes, Harper?" Miss Grinter asked, with surprise in her tone.

The class turned around to look. Two thin shards of light streaked through the blind at the window and lay across Harper's face. Freckles lightly decorated her abnormally high cheekbones and black, thick-rimmed glasses tried, but failed, to hide her sparkling blue eyes. The long hair that most people would use as a trophy, was used, by Harper, as more of a blanket. It was thick, glossy, and cascaded down her chest.

"So, there is such a thing as objective beauty?" she asked.

"Erm well, yes," Miss Grinter replied.

Miss Grinter continued explaining the plan for the lesson and the class turned back to face the front and receive the instructions. All except Jesse. He continued looking at Harper who, since asking the question, had begun writing something down in her notebook. He was intrigued by the idea of the golden ratio and, for the first time, he was intrigued by Harper.

Eventually the bell rang to indicate the end of class and the students filed out into the crowded corridor.

Jesse jogged to catch up with Harper who was always quick to leave a class. He approached her and whacked her, a little harder than he had intended, on the shoulder.

"What?" Harper spun round to see who she was addressing the question to.

"Nice to meet you, too," said Jesse.

"Meet? We've been in the same class for nearly five years, Jesse," Harper said with a sigh.

"Ah, yes, but we've never really spoken, have we?"

"And all of a sudden you've got something to say to me?"

"What were your thoughts on the golden ratio?" he asked.

"You heard them. I said what I was thinking in class," said Harper.

"I heard what you were willing to share with the class. I didn't hear what you then wrote down in your little notebook," he said, giving her a quick flash of his smile.

"I wrote down what I said and what Miss Grinter replied," said Harper with a completely straight face.

"Bullshit. Show me," said Jesse, sticking out his hand for her to pass him the notebook.

Harper took half a step back from Jesse as they continued standing in the corridor while students filed past them. She looked down at his hand which he quickly moved back by his side, then looked up at him.

"You're genuinely interested in my thoughts on the golden ratio?" she finally asked.

"I am genuinely interested in your thoughts on the golden ratio, yes," said Jesse.

"Get stuffed," said Harper.

She began to walk off.

Jesse ran after her, jumped in front of her and stopped.

"I'm going to create objective beauty and sell it," he blurted out.

Harper adjusted her bag on her shoulder and looked intently at Jesse for the first time. She looked up at his shining curls, then looked down over his baggy school trousers, to his shining leather shoes, then back up directly into his eyes.

"Meet me after school in the library," she said. "I'll show you what I wrote."

"The library? I've never stepped foot in that place. I can't go in there it's for—"

But she was not listening and had already walked off.

Chapter Three

"What on Earth am I doing?" Jesse muttered to himself as he approached the grand library steps, the wide slabs of stone absorbing the remaining heat of the late-afternoon sun.

He had never been to this place voluntarily before. It was full of people who were not like him and who would never be like him. As he looked around at the unfamiliar scene, his mind began to wander.

What if Harper's just winding me up, he thought. *She clearly doesn't like me. She has no reason to. I've never invited her to a party. Or acknowledged her existence. What if I've just handed her an opportunity to trick me?*

Jesse was convinced by his own thoughts and had just decided to walk off and keep his reputation intact, when a student who was also in their maths class stepped out of the front door and jogged lightly down the steps while putting her arms through the sleeves of her blazer.

Jesse caught her eye.

She stopped on the penultimate step and returned Jesse's gaze.

"Harper's waiting for you in there," she said with a short nod, then buttoned up her blazer and walked off.

"Thanks," said Jesse, too late to be heard.

He dropped his shoulders, let out a deep sigh, and looked again at the library. There was one thing he had to admit. It was a beautiful building. The complex design and beautiful stone carvings told the story of a time when intricacy was prioritised over efficiency...

Jesse caught himself.

Imagine if someone could hear your thoughts right now, he reprimanded himself. *You're an embarrassment. Just go inside and get what you need from that geek, Harper.*

He pulled his shirt collar up around his neck, put his hands in his trouser pockets, walked up the steps two at a time, and entered the library.

It was full of books. Jesse could not help that his first reaction was one that so simply stated the obvious. He had only ever read books that he had been forced to read at school – science textbooks, To Kill A Mockingbird, French revision flashcards, GCSE poetry anthologies – and he had not even bothered to read most of those the whole way through.

"Hi, can I, I don't have a card," Jesse muttered to the librarian who sat at the desk in the main room. He shoved his hands deeper into his pockets while he spoke.

The librarian looked up at Jesse, her eyes peering over the top rim of her glasses.

"That's okay," she said, lifting her head up then removing her glasses with one hand. "You don't need a card to go in, only to take out books." She smiled.

"Thanks," muttered Jesse, feeling instantly stupid in front of this serene lady.

He walked toward the group study desks to look for Harper.

There was an unusual smell in the library. It was old and musty yet new and intriguing at the same time. He reached out and gently touched the spine of a book as he walked alongside the many volumes on the shelves. He wondered how many other hands had touched that spine before him. He wondered how many minds had been deeply, profoundly affected by the words in the books. They had shelves of books at home, but his dad was never in the house to read them, and his mum was mostly too drunk to read anything.

Then he saw her, sitting at one of the large wooden desks. Her blazer was on the back of the chair and her white shirt was sticking out from beneath her thin, navy blue school jumper. She sat with her right foot tucked under her left thigh on the chair and was writing on a piece of lined paper.

Jesse walked up to her desk and stood in front of it.

"Ahem," Jesse coughed to get Harper's attention.

She lifted her head, unable to hide the surprise in her smile.

"Sit down," she said, pointing at the chair opposite her.

Jesse sat down, shuffled on the plastic chair, and pulled it in to get comfy. The lamp between them threw a warm light on their faces.

"What are you working on?" Jesse asked while gently tapping the edge of the desk.

"Well, seeing as you are here to talk to me about the golden ratio, I will admit I was making more notes on my plans for the golden ratio," she said, talking carefully and in a very matter of fact tone.

Jesse liked the precision of her voice and the gentle notes were far from the high energy deluge of his mates that he was used to.

"I just wanted to know what you wrote down after asking if there is such thing as objective beauty in class. I didn't necessarily come here to discuss the matter further than that."

"I will tell you what I wrote if you tell me why you are so interested," said Harper. "You must have some thoughts for yourself?"

"You tell me first," Jesse smiled, "and then I'll decide whether or not to tell you my thoughts."

Harper looked at Jesse. It was a terrible offer but endearingly honest and Jesse had something about him, an energy, that Harper wanted to spend more time with. So, she obliged and, with no further questioning, began to read from her notes. The notes she had written mid-maths lesson.

Chapter Four

Ax and the fairy opposite nodded hello to each other at the dining table.

"Would you pass me the water?" Ax asked him.

The fairy must have been only a year older than Ax, perhaps eighteen, but the lines around his eyes and his thick eyebrows could have made him older. There were many fairies in the dining hall during a mealtime. They sat wherever the next empty seat was and so were almost always seated next to someone they did not know.

"Still or sparkling?" the fairy replied.

"Sparkling. Thanks," said Ax, reaching to collect the bottle halfway across the table. "I'm Ax," he added.

"Everyone knows who you are," the fairy said with a warm smile.

Ax often received this response. Not only was he son of The Kingdom's godmother, but his damaged wing was a distinguishing feature. Nevertheless, he did not know how else to introduce himself, so he still always started by offering his name.

"I'm Sivas," said Sivas.

The two fairies leant forward and shook hands across the table, careful not to knock over any bottles or glasses in the process.

"Is it true that you don't have a human?" Sivas asked, sitting back down.

"It's true," nodded Ax.

"So, how does that work? How do you find a purpose without having a human to look after?" he asked.

Ax was enjoying Sivas's confidence. Other fairies did not usually dare ask questions like this, even after knowing him for a while. It felt refreshing to be with a fairy who was not intimidated by him.

"I still go down to Earth," said Ax. "I still watch humans."

"Is it true that when you do go down to Earth you can't stay there for long?"

"Yeah," said Ax. He sat up a bit straighter, put his spoon down on a napkin, and turned his shoulders slightly to the side. "This wing is too weak to get me back up if my energy drains too much."

Sivas looked sufficiently impressed at the famous wings. Ax smiled, straightened up, and picked his spoon back up.

"If you ever need help, I'm your friend now," said Sivas.

Ax looked at him. It was Ax's first ever proper offer of friendship and he was going to take it.

"Thanks, I'll remember that," said Ax.

The first course was over and, when the soup bowls were cleared, the vegetarian shepherd's pie arrived with a crispy, cheesy topping, more warm bread, and an option of black tea or coffee with cream.

There were many misconceptions about The Kingdom held by other fairy lands and one such falsity was that fairies in The Kingdom only ate gold flakes, which was absurd and untrue. Fairies in all lands did not *need* to eat at all, but for as long as The Kingdom fairies could remember they had sat down to eat human-replica food once a day. It was one of the few rituals they thought was done rather well on Earth. Fairies liked hot, savoury dishes from all over the planet, often spicy ones. They were not really fussed about sweet food and were all vegetarians.

Some fairy lands didn't eat or drink. Some didn't eat but *did* drink. The Amett Land fairies famously only drank freshly ground black coffee. But in The Kingdom fairies ate and drank together. Maye often jokingly gave the daily ritual credit for why The Kingdom remained the most powerful of all within the fairy realm.

Lorkun Lodge was incredibly powerful, too. It had been the first fairy land to break off from The Kingdom almost one hundred thousand years ago. Axone had always predicted a future in which Lorkun Lodge was defeated, but few other fairies shared his hopeful vision and, when Axone died, many fairies who believed him ceased to, and it became harder to convince others.

So, the lands remained divided. Fairies of The Kingdom strove to free the humans from their Earthly obsessions and Earthly fears; while fairies of Lorkun Lodge continued to tempt the humans with possessions and fantasies that lured the humans into a false sense of control. Ax had always struggled with this.

"Why do they tell the humans that freedom is being able to get what you want?" a young, frustrated Ax had cried to his mother when he arrived home from his first week of school after learning what the Lorkun fairies are trained to do. "It's so obvious, Mum, that it's not true. They're making the humans suffer needlessly."

"I know my baby," said Maye, stroking his hair, allowing his small tears to sink into her white cotton dress. "It feels so unfair," she said softly to herself as well as to her son.

"What even is suffering, Mum?" he asked, looking up at her.

"It is necessary," said Maye, "and it reminds humans they are not in their true home."

They closed their eyes and Maye continued to stroke her son's hair while he sat on her lap, until eventually he fell asleep with his head on her chest.

The meal was finished, and the port was being poured into each glass thimble on the table. Filling them all was a feat that took mere seconds thanks to the skilled fairy waiters who poured themselves one too.

The fairies in the room raised their glasses in unison and the chorus began, some singing, some speaking, all in a wide range of tones. It was a beautiful sound:

"To the protection and release of humans who were all born to create. I will drink this and commit to sharing my energy and love with them."

They briefly stretched their thimbles one inch higher, clinked them together with a dazzling, rippling melody of tinkles, before bringing them back to their mouth and downing the sweet red liquid in one gulp.

Sivas and Ax put their empty thimbles on the table and glanced at each other as they stood up to leave.

"Nice to meet you," said Ax.

"Hey, do you want to come with me to the conservatory?" Sivas asked while Ax tucked in his chair. "I'm just going over to look at the fruit trees now. I often water them."

Ax paused. "Yeah. That sounds nice," he said.

He waited for Sivas to reach him and they travelled to the trees together.

They arrived at the conservatory, a one-thousand-acre collection of greenhouses, raised flower beds, and lines of various fruit trees. They began filling up the watering cans. Ax thought about the fact that he had never really done an activity with another fairy before. Not without it being arranged by fairy school. His high status in The Kingdom meant he was regularly alone. But Sivas did not mind the hierarchy gap and Ax was thrilled.

"They have these apple trees down on Earth," said Sivas. "I take it you've been to see them?"

"I've seen some. I've seen lots of plants. I've never eaten an Earth fruit though. I've only ever eaten fairy fruit from the conservatory here, especially draigon fruit. They should have that on Earth, honestly."

"Ah, I'll have to take you to my favourite apple tree on Earth then, won't I?" said Sivas. "There's one in my human's garden and there's a few in the school right below us."

"I've seen that one," said Ax. "I watch two humans in that school."

"Marlborough High School? I love it there. Let's go together tomorrow," said Sivas, pausing the watering and standing up straight.

"Okay," said Ax, continuing to water.

He knew that he would have to lay low until then and get some rest. He'd had a close call, exhausting nearly all his energy on Earth today, and going back down tomorrow would require more rest than usual which could appear suspicious if Maye noticed. But he didn't want Sivas to know he had to go through such boring restraints which most fairies their age never had to consider.

"Meet me by the entrance and we'll go down together tomorrow at eleven a.m." said Sivas.

"I'll be there," said Ax, trying to decide whether this new feeling was excitement or fear.

Chapter Five

Harper and Jesse were still sitting opposite each other at the desk, surrounded by the whispers of fellow students working in groups in the library.

Harper finished reading, shut the well-worn notebook with a snap, and pushed it to the side of the desk.

Jesse leant back in his chair, the legs creaking slightly beneath him, but did not say a word.

Then Harper pulled five sheets of A4 from a clear plastic wallet and spread them out over the desk, her intricate inky writing covering each page. She adjusted the desk lamp to shine on the papers, pushed her glasses further up her nose, then peered up at Jesse to see what he was looking at. He was looking at her.

"So," Harper began, looking quickly back down at her papers. "If there's such thing as objective beauty, which can be discovered and created with some simple maths," she continued, "then it could be utilised to make millions."

Jesse dropped his shoulders and sat up, annoyed.

"Right, dumbo," he whispered as loud as he could. "So, state the flipping obvious in your conclusion. But you can't just sell a maths formula. Don't you think if you could sell it, it would have been done by now? And besides, it's not our– it's not *yours* to sell."

Harper carried on looking at the papers. She continued explaining.

"Of course, many people know about it, and many people will be using it in art, architecture, fashion…" She trailed off looking up at the ceiling, and Jesse felt an insatiable urge to know what she was thinking. She looked back down. "But many will be doing it unknowingly and the rest will be doing it without knowing how to monetise it."

"So, how are you going to monetise it?" he asked.

"Well, that I'm going to keep to myself," Harper said politely. "But I am glad you had some interest in it and you're welcome to ask me more questions when the project is running in, I guess, a few months' time."

Harper looked at Jesse. She pushed her glasses up her nose, as she was in the habit of doing.

Jesse didn't know what to do. Harper had clearly just finished the conversation.

"That's it? That's all you want to say to me? I've come all this way and that's all I get to hear?" he asked.

"I'm sorry, I didn't know I owed you something. I've told you what I wrote in the maths lesson."

Jesse's jaw tightened. He couldn't understand why she was doing this to him. She had just been so generous with her time. Why was she not sharing her project?

He pushed back his chair and stood up to leave.

"Your idea is bullshit," he said, getting the attention of the students on the next table. "What?" he said to the students who duly got back to their work.

He put his coat on, tucked his chair back in, looked at Harper, shook his head, forcing his curls to move, and walked off.

She watched him walk away.

Jesse stood at the top of the library steps at the front of the building and fired off five texts to Mark.

"Just been to see that geek in the library – I actually thought she might be cool – But she's got nothing to say – It's so obvious I'm smarter than her – Meet me at the pub for a drink?"

"The library?!" Mark replied. "We're in the White Horse."

Jesse trotted down the steps and went off to meet his mates, the frustration, at least, distracting him from the slight drop in temperature.

Chapter Six

The next morning Jesse queued for a freeze-dried economy coffee and a microwaved croissant from the school's cafeteria before lessons began. Harper walked in after him, a muddled mass of papers under her arms. She walked across the room in her black leather shoes with an air of confidence that emanated, not from being cool, but from her self-assured disregard for what people considered cool.

She walked up to the counter and ordered a cup of sweet, milky tea behind Jesse who had just ordered his sugarless black coffee. They glanced quickly at each other, but then both turned to face the counter. They didn't say a word.

Jesse took his change and his breakfast from the dinner lady and sat at one of the canteen tables which were all a little too small for his seventeen-year-old frame, and concentrated on the soggy croissant which lay on the plastic plate in front of him.

He had left Harper in a rush the day before and knew he had reacted unfairly. He liked her and wanted them to be friends. He was intrigued by her golden ratio plan but did not know how to tell her that. He could chat up a girl, *any* girl, no problem. He sometimes did it just for fun, even if he didn't like them. He knew those girls saw his bouncing curls, smooth skin, and high energy, and instantly placed him higher than themselves in an imagined social hierarchy. They then acted as though the social positions were real for the remaining time in which they knew him.

Harper was different to those girls. It meant some people thought she lacked social skills, but Jesse was getting to know her now and he was starting to become intrigued by her slight detachment from reality.

He was still thinking about Harper when she walked up to the low grey table and sat down opposite him, her tea dancing at the rim of the cup as she placed it down.

"Hi," he said.

"Do you want to hear the rest of my golden ratio plan?" she asked, not wasting any time.

"I thought I— I don't know— I mean yeah, I would love that," he said, putting one hand into his curls and absentmindedly scratching the side of his head.

Harper smiled. "I need to know you're serious about keeping this between us for now, though. There may be a lot of money involved eventually," she said.

Jesse looked at her with wide eyes and spoke with a hushed voice. "I don't know how to prove I'm being sincere," he said, leaning a little closer so she could hear. "Other than the fact I turned up at a flipping library yesterday in public where anyone could have seen me. Just to speak to you about it."

"I was surprised you actually turned up," she smiled.

"What can I do?" he asked, not smiling back.

"Tell me your plan."

"*My* plan for the golden ratio?"

"Yeah," she said. "If you're so interested in what I have to say about it, you must have some thoughts for yourself."

Jesse looked at Harper. Harper looked at Jesse.

"Not here," said Jesse with a quick shake of his head. He took a sip of the thin, watery coffee. "Can you meet me tonight?"

"Come to my parents' house if you want," she said.

Jesse looked unsure.

"Oh, yeah, sorry I forgot, you can't be seen to be hanging out with a geek like me," she said. "No worries."

"No, no, no," Jesse caught himself. "It's just that I'm meeting Mark later. I'll come over before I see him. Seven-thirty?"

***

Jesse hit the silver knocker against the red paint that flaked off from the door of Harper's Victorian terraced house. This part of town was different to the area in which Jesse lived. He never came to this side of the city where cramped houses and high-rise flats replaced private, detached mansions; where car alarms replaced birdsong; and where the smell of greasy, thin burgers replaced steaming hot, home-made lasagne. He heard shouting from the bus stop down the road while he waited and made a mental note to get a taxi home later.

Harper appeared at the door.

"Come in," she said with a smile, holding the door wide open. She was wearing dark blue, fitted jeans, a cropped black fluffy jumper, and brown, faux-fur lined slippers. "You can put your bag on the floor there and your coat on the hook there," she said, pointing while she spoke.

They walked into the kitchen together and sat at the cluttered table. Harper pushed three toy cars and a dirty mug to the side then lit the red candle, which had dripped wax onto the wood the last time it had been used.

There was a momentary silence as they looked at the flickering flame.

"Look, I'm not going to stay long," said Jesse, "But I think the golden ratio can be sold."

"That's because I told you that?" asked Harper.

"No, I thought it even before I met you," he insisted. "I thought it before I approached you in the corridor. Before I met you in the library. Before I got to find out what you had written down."

"Right," she said, pushing her glasses up on her nose. "And that's your only thought on the matter?"

"No. I also think it could be sold to make people become beautiful. And it could make us millionaires."

"People already are beautiful," she said.

He looked at her. "Everybody wants to be. And everyone is on the inside. But we could make them beautiful on the outside."

"If we did that, then wouldn't beauty become pointless?"

"No." Jesse had thought this through. "Has anyone ever got bored of a rainbow? Has anyone ever, in the *whole wide world,* looked at a sunset and thought it looked just 'okay'?"

"Just checking," said Harper, "that you know what you're talking about before I give you more of my ideas."

She reached down, pulled a stack of papers out of her school satchel, and put them in front of her.

Jesse moved one seat closer to her so he could see better. He looked at the top of one of the pages and read the words aloud written in Harper's inky letters.

"Sell beauty," he said.

He continued scanning her notes. Underneath 'sell beauty' it said, 'surgery or pill or make-up. It could make millions.' There was a large question mark beneath it, and some phone numbers below that.

He stared at the words then looked up as Harper passed him another sheet of paper. The sheet had faces she had drawn on it. Children's faces, teenage faces, adult faces, and older faces. They were all designed using the golden ratio to find the proportion for the features. Next to the faces were hands. Each joint from the tips of the fingers, and all the way up to the wrist, had a pencilled diagram on top to show they were drawn using the golden ratio.

Jesse put it down in front of him and continued to look at the other sheets. He tilted his head as he pulled out another page from within the pile. It was filled with more writing. It had pros and cons, it had sums and figures, it had age limits, it had surgery phone numbers, it had knives that she had drawn. 'Injections' was written at the bottom of the page and it had been underlined three times in red felt tip.

"What are the phone numbers?" Jesse asked.

"Surgeons."

"Have you spoken to any of them?" he asked.

Harper hesitated then went and closed the kitchen door, leaning on it gently until she heard it click. She walked to the fridge and poured them both a tumbler of orange juice, placed the glasses on the coaster-less table in front of them, and sat back down.

She took a sip of her drink.

"I have spoken to a lot. All of them said no," she said.

Jesse raised his eyebrows. "You mean they didn't take a schoolgirl seriously about a life-changing, brand new, million-dollar injection?"

Harper pursed her lips.

"So, we just need to find more to phone," he said.

"Except one," said Harper. "One plastic surgeon thinks it can be done. He lives in L.A., so I emailed him. He listened to me because he knows me. He's my mum's brother."

Jesse's eyes glanced back at the words 'Uncle Henry?' on the piece of paper.

"Uncle Henry," she continued, catching the line of Jesse's gaze. "He hasn't been to the UK for seventeen years."

"What did he say?" asked Jesse.

"Are you serious about this?"

Jesse looked at her and nodded, his eyes not leaving hers.

"This doesn't leave these walls," said Harper.

"Okay," said Jesse.

"There's one more thing before I tell you this," she said. "He knows the Headmaster."

"Our Headmaster?" he asked.

Harper paused with a confused frown. "Yes," she said.

"Alright," he said.

Harper picked up her phone, tapped in the six-digit password, and opened her emails. She found the first email from Uncle Henry. She began to read.

Hello, Harper!

I can't believe it's you. Your Aunt and I have known for a while that this could happen. Your Headmaster was adamant we waited for the right student to take interest without any manipulation and how right he turned out to be! Although, he won't talk to you about it. He'll leave that to me. And I am SO pleased it is my own niece! Now, I dare say you are already thinking me a little nutty on reading this email opening. I will be able to explain more soon. Did your mother tell you I am visiting over the Christmas period? By the

way, does she know you have sent me this? It may be better that she doesn't know about it. Not yet. Let's arrange a phone call. I have some answers for those questions you have asked and a lot more to tell you, as well! It will be safe to discuss on the phone.

Let me know a good time to call.

Much love,

Your Uncle H.

"I phoned him straight away. He told me about an injection on which he has been working for seventeen years," said Harper when she finished reading the email and put her phone face-down on the kitchen table. "He told me he's known the Headmaster since before I was born. I had no idea."

Jesse's eyes were wide. "Why doesn't the Headmaster want to talk to us about it?" he asked.

"I don't know," said Harper.

"Right. What sort of injections?" asked Jesse.

Harper shuffled on her chair. "They're mixture of lip filler and Botox. Bizarrely, they have not yet been combined," she said and began lightly wiping at the condensation that had appeared on the side of her glass with her fingers. "There can be some strange side effects." She wiped her fingers on her jeans and took a sip of her cold drink. "And then there is one more chemical that needs to be added which has never been commercially incorporated and has never caused harm in animals but has not made it to the popular market with plastic surgeons in this country yet either."

"Why not?" asked Jesse.

"The side effects."

"I thought you said it didn't cause any harm in the animals."

"Not *harm*," said Harper. "But changes. It made them more confident. It made them smarter. It made them feel on top of the world. Uncle Henry thinks it is because it made them see beauty in everything."

"And what is wrong with that?!" asked Jesse furrowing his brow slightly.

"It's hard to explain."

"I think you'd better at least try to explain it."

Harper took a deep breath and pulled her left leg up onto the chair beneath her right thigh. She relaxed her shoulders and began to speak.

"The formula will make a person beautiful in line with the golden ratio. It is a liquid chemical that will make you beautiful when injected into the perfect place on your face. There is a side effect to the injection, though. It also means you're able to see only beauty around you. That's the bit that excites Uncle Henry: when a person can see only beauty around them, and are incredibly beautiful themselves, the whole structure of society falls apart and all power and control, which some people have over others, is lost. He believes that we are being kept in our 'place' by whether we perceive ourselves as beautiful or not. Based on our assumption of our own beauty, and of the beauty around us, we *choose* our level of power, authority, and control. We *choose* what we can and cannot experience based on assumptions we've made about our own beauty and the beauty of other people and things around us. We don't realise we're doing it, but we're putting ourselves in a specific position within social hierarchies, determining what we will then attract and experience."

Jesse opened his mouth to speak, furrowed his brow, then closed his mouth again.

Harper smiled and continued.

"Uncle Henry said the Headmaster also knows all of this. He also explained that if someone uses too much of the chemical formula in the injection, or does something morally wrong while under the influence, there is potential for this going very wrong. It's why no-one has been brave enough to pursue the project with them yet, despite the money-making potential and obvious benefits for the human race. He said he and the Headmaster have been convinced they need someone with the energy of youth and a natural interest in the topic to help them. He said that, finally, the product is ready to be launched."

"It definitely shows that he's from L.A.," said Jesse, letting out a huge sigh and leaning back slightly on his chair.

"You don't have to be here," said Harper. "If you think it's airy-fairy nonsense." She started collecting her papers together.

"I've got to get back home," he said, checking the time on his phone, then realised he had not touched his orange juice and lifted it for a long swig. "Pizza and beer with Mark tonight and it's already eight o'clock. If I don't show up it will raise suspicions and he will ask questions that I really don't want to have to answer right now."

"Jesse. If you *are* serious about this, we can do it together, with Uncle Henry and the

Headmaster," she said softly, not commenting on the priorities he had just chosen. "The money we will make could be incredible. And we will be doing everybody a favour. I trust my uncle, even if you don't."

Jesse was a little overwhelmed by what Harper was saying and the potential impact was far beyond what he had imagined.

"Weirdly I think I trust your uncle, too," he said. "I just need time to think."

"Alright," said Harper.

Jesse went back out into the hallway, put on his coat, and picked up his bag.

"You have my word on the secret," he said when Harper opened the front door. "Whatever I decide, if anyone finds out, it will not be from me. My lips are sealed."

And then he left.

Chapter Seven

Ax and Sivas met in The Kingdom's front lobby as planned.

"Where are we going first?" Ax asked his new friend.

"Oxford. You been before?"

"No," said Ax.

"Son of The Kingdom's godmother and you've not even lived enough to see the beautiful city of Oxford," Sivas chuckled, affectionately.

Ax looked down at his feet and forced a small laugh.

"You'll be telling me you haven't seen London next," said Sivas.

"My wings couldn't really handle the flight. It's too far," Ax explained.

"Oh goodness, you are kidding. Okay, that's where we're going today then. And don't worry, you're with me so no matter where we go you will be able to get back up," said Sivas.

"It's nice to have someone to travel with," said Ax.

"Let's go," said Sivas.

The two fairies swooped down from The Kingdom and into Earth's atmosphere. They headed right over Marlborough High School.

"That's where the two teenagers I watch go," Ax told Sivas as they flew over the old building's red slate tiles and large slabs of luminous Bath stone.

"I know, you said!" Sivas reminded him. "One of my humans has dated a few girls there. He also travels to Oxford and London a lot. Hence where I'm showing you today. I know the two cities like the back of my hand."

They flew through Earth's atmosphere for the next bit of the journey, then, once they were above Oxford, they descended into the grounds of one of the University's colleges. It was a slightly newer building than most, away from the main hustle of the city. The grass in the courtyard was messy and lived in, in contrast to the prepped and preened grass found in other parts of the historic town.

"One of the newest colleges built for the University," said Sivas. "Recently celebrated their 67th anniversary."

"Nice," said Ax.

While stepping into the courtyard, Ax felt his stomach tighten and turn. A small shiver hit the back of his neck and he rolled his shoulders back to ease it.

He wondered whether he had already used too much energy.

"Nice, huh?" asked Sivas, flying in quick circles for fun.

"I feel as though I know it," said Ax.

"Yeah," said Sivas. "It's filled with graduates from over ninety countries and is the only college at the University not to have a high table."

"What's a high table?" asked Ax.

"Horrendous things where the important people sit for dinner. Other diners stand up when the important ones walk in for their meal."

Sivas was whizzing around again, enjoying the warm day.

Ax flew onto a picnic bench and had a flashback of being curled up in his mother's womb. The fleeting image disappeared.

"I mean I really feel as though I've been here," said Ax.

He flew up off the wooden slats over to Sivas by the dining hall. They went into the library, up the soft, red carpeted stairs, then out onto the slanted college roof.

"I can see a fairy," Ax said when they were outside. "There! On top of the flagpole. He's about to fall!"

Ax's palms began sweating and his chest tightened. He put his hand on his ribcage where he felt his muscles pull and pressed down gently with the palm of his hand.

"Are you okay? There's nothing there. You're seeing things," Sivas laughed and flew off. "Come on."

"There was," said Ax under his breath but Sivas had gone. He moved his hand, pleased the uncomfortable sensation in his chest had loosened.

Maybe Sivas was right, Ax thought. Maybe he had lost the plot. But he had definitely seen something there. He definitely had.

"We'll come back here," said Sivas. "I just wanted to swing by quickly. I have lots more to show you here but let's go back up and along to London now."

They remained in Earth's atmosphere as they headed towards London. Ax was starting to feel tired but didn't say anything. He could feel himself slowing down and tried to adopt the air of someone who was simply relaxed and enjoying a slower journey rather than someone who could not go any faster. He decided he would say something if it got worse. He would just make sure they didn't remain in London too long. By now Ax knew what it felt like to have his energy drained. Plus, it would be even easier now that he had Sivas to help him.

They reached London and headed down towards street level, flying at the same height as most of the concrete roofs.

Ax started to cough.

Sivas looked over at him.

"Pollution," said Sivas from a few metres to the side, chuckling. "Here, catch this."

He pulled a white piece of cloth from his pocket and threw it across the air to Ax as they travelled over the Thames.

"It's a facemask," he called once Ax caught it.

"Thanks," said Ax, tying the sides of the cloth at the back of his head. "How do the humans breathe down here?" he asked.

"This isn't even as far down as it goes," said Sivas. "They have an underground travel system here. If you think it's hard to breathe now you ought to go down there."

"No thanks," said Ax with a straight face and raised eyebrows.

"This is Tower Bridge," said Sivas as they approached impressive structure that straddled the river.

They landed on top of the large blue metal railings, regained their composure, and looked around. Murky water flowed beneath them and trees blew gently back and forth at the edge of the river while two ducks fought over a small scrap of bread.

"So, this is London," said Ax. "It's busy."

"Understatement," said Sivas.

"Oh, gosh." Ax jumped slightly at the sight to his right. "Why is that man throwing up green vomit?" he asked, his voice wobbling slightly with panic.

Ax flew closer to the man.

"And no one is stopping to help him? They're just all walking past as though nothing is going on at all. He's throwing up over and over. What is that?" Ax asked.

"That's rejection," said Sivas flying to join Ax.

"What?"

"The others can't see it. The other humans can't see it. The man who's vomiting doesn't know he's vomiting either."

"He's literally puking up copious amounts of green slime," Ax could not believe what he was seeing. "How can no one notice that?"

"They don't see it. But believe me, the man who is vomiting is feeling it."

"Ouch," said Ax. "That has got to hurt."

"It's one of the most painful feelings a human can go through," said Sivas.

"What sort of rejection can trigger it?" asked Ax.

"Oh, anything. A stranger not moving their bag on the bus for you. Not having a photo liked on social media. Those are mild ones though. From the amount he's vomiting, I'd say it might have been a relationship break-up."

"Wow."

"They can vomit for weeks and months on end after something like that. Same thing after a death. It is intensely painful and can be so strenuous on the body that some don't always fully recover from it."

"Don't they have any medicine to help?" asked Ax, knowing that humans were proficient at medicating.

"Like I said, they don't know they're doing it. They might eat more sugar to increase their energy, or drink alcohol to dissolve the pain momentarily. Some might meditate. But the fact is, whatever they do to help themselves, all the green vomit must come out. There isn't a healthy person who hasn't removed the green slime of rejection completely by vomiting. Some choose not to throw it up because they can't handle the pain, so they just carry on with the slime inside them. But it's toxic. It builds up and hardens until eventually they cannot be loved. The most efficient humans just throw it all up in one night! But that is dangerous. It takes a lot of practice as well as a fair bit of bravery."

"Goodness. I never imagined it to feel that bad. And how strange that they can't see it," said Ax.

"There's lots that they can't see," said Sivas.

"Like us, for example," said Ax, letting out a small sigh.

He always felt sad that humans couldn't see fairies because it meant so many humans refused to believe they existed.

"And hate, anger, love, they can't see any of it," added Sivas. "Some of them can feel it, though. And some of them allow themselves to feel it more than others."

The man who was vomiting had disappeared and Sivas and Ax continued travelling around. Ax was starting to really like Sivas.

"Right let's get back up," said Sivas. "I don't want to get in trouble with your mum."

"Oh, she'll be fine but, well, yeah, we better get back up," said Ax.

Sivas, who could tell Ax's energy was getting low, gave Ax a ride back up.

They reached The Kingdom just as the dinner bell began to ring.

"I'm going the long way round," said Sivas. "I want to go down there again with you. I have so much more to show you."

"Okay," said Ax with a nod. "I will look forward to that."

78

Ax went off to dinner feeling warm. He was excited. He was also distracted. So much so that even when a beautiful fairy asked him to pass the butter during dinner, a clear sign that she wanted to get to know him, he stayed in his inward daze, thinking about the new world of humans he'd seen and the green vomit that was all over London. He had never seen that on any of his brief visits to Marlborough High to watch Harper and Jesse.

Chapter Eight

Ax flew over the soft golden carpets that ran the length of the corridors. He flew towards his mum's personal room, where a warm light was spilling out from under the door. He had been feeling guilty about sneaking around on Earth with Sivas and wanted to go and see her. He pulled back his broken wing and slipped in under the door.

"My baby, please don't do that," said Maye with a twinkle in her eye, looking at her son with mock surprise.

One of the benefits to having a broken wing was that he could fit through tight spaces and sneak up on his mum and the Elders.

He sat on the dark green velvet sofa and watched as Maye pressed a golden, shimmering powder onto her eyelids, then brushed light through her hair. Her eyes twinkled. Her skin was smooth. She appeared ageless, despite having been through more than a lifetime's worth of pain.

When Axone died fairies worried how Maye would grieve and love simultaneously when her baby was born. Yet, since the day Axone Junior arrived she had governed with grace, always fair to others, even when life was not fair to her. She could heal. One touch of her smooth hand could cure any fairy illness or injury. It was a gift she acquired after her father died.

The only illness or injury she had not healed since then was Ax's wing.

"Well, mama, you wouldn't heal my wing, so it means I'm going to be able to sneak up on you all the time," he said, flying over to the mirror and wrapping his arms around his mum's shoulders to show he was teasing her.

But it was a difficult subject for Maye.

"It's not so simple, Ax. You know that," she said, breathing in his smell, wondering when his odour had changed from talcum powder and lightly perfumed baby wipes into a rich pine aftershave and cold moisturising cream.

"I don't see why I can't just have two good wings," he said. "Then I'd be able to have my own human and everything. I'd be able to go to Earth for as long as I want."

"It was your grandfather's wing. You inherited it through war," she replied, a cautious smile on her face.

Ax had heard the story a million times. He flew to his mother's glossy white mantelpiece and made himself a Bloody Mary: vodka, tomato juice, black pepper, and a lot of lemon. Vodka was another one of the Earthly human pleasures that fairies dabbled in for fun, even when they were only seventeen.

"One day," said Maye, now sitting on the top of her desk, looking at her son who was flying to the window with a drink in his hand, "you will understand how much pain the decision caused me and you will understand why I had to do it."

"So cryptic, Mum! Come on. Don't worry. You know I don't really care."

Maye smiled at her son.

"Besides, if you fixed my wing, I'd only have one human and you'll never guess what – the two humans I watch have come together. They even seem to even be getting on."

He took a large swig of his drink and fluttered up to the top of the window.

"You have the most intrigue and love for humans I have ever known. Only your grandfather has ever had the same." Maye looked proudly at her son. "I am so proud of you. But, Ax," she paused.

"Yes, Mum?"

"Don't be spending too much time on Earth. You know your wing makes you— You know you can't do all the things the other fairies can do, don't you?"

"Yes mum, I'm not immortal. It's okay, you can say it."

"Just be careful," she said.

She flew over to him and put her hand on his. "I love you," she said.

Ax gave his mum a kiss on the cheek and flew to the door.

Maye opened it and, as Ax flew out, the Elders arrived.

"He has the energy of his grandfather," she said as they came in.

"Are you ever going to tell him what you know?" asked Elba.

Maye was quiet, a solemnity filling the room.

"I can't," she said.

"Don't you think he has a right to know?" asked Elba.

"It's not certain that it will happen. I'm not certain that I will allow it to happen," she said.

"Even if it causes the destruction of humans on Earth?" asked Elson.

"How can I ever choose between my humans and my son?" asked Maye.

"I think you're forgetting, Maye, that in the end it might not be your choice," added Elrin.

She understood this with as much clarity now as she had done in the moments following Ax's birth, when they were taken into the out-of-bounds room and discovered what her son had been born with and the complications around his future. In fact, it had never once fully left her mind.

Chapter Nine

"You've got to get back down on Earth. It doesn't matter if she's saying that," said Sivas.

Sivas was hovering up and down over his chair, talking to Ax with a chunk of bread in his mouth, feeling restless at the dinner table.

"There's a lot of London I still want to show you," he continued.

Ax could feel the allure. He had told Sivas, at the beginning of dinner, that his mum had said he shouldn't be going to Earth too much, and Sivas was not taking it well. Ax had wanted Sivas to be right and his mum to be wrong. He had become obsessed with the idea of visiting London again since seeing it for the first time. While Sivas continued talking Ax drifted into his thoughts. His mum meant he should not go down *alone.* It wouldn't be ideal but travelling with Sivas would not be life threatening. Maye didn't need to worry so much.

"Are you listening?" Sivas asked.

"Yeah, sorry," said Ax. "I think it's a good idea. My mum will be fine. She just worries, you know."

"Great!" said Sivas, smearing a large lump of butter onto what remained of his bread roll in celebration.

Ax was pretty sure his mum had meant he simply should not go alone, but recently he had also been wondering whether she knew more than he realised about his latest excursions. He was sure there was a way of his mum and the Elders watching him. They always seemed to know everything about the fairies in The Kingdom and, while Maye would never tell him explicitly what to do, she had been hinting more than normal that he ought to stay safe.

"Besides, I do want to see more in London," said Ax.

"I think it will help you understand your humans more," said Sivas. "What are they called again?"

"Jesse and Harper. And they're not my humans—"

"Yeah, yeah you don't have a specific human you just watch them all and love them all. I know, I know," said Sivas, flying around again.

The meal was coming to an end and the fortified wine was being poured into the thimbles.

"Do you know Madinal?" Sivas asked, leaning back slightly while his glass was filled.

"I don't think so," said Ax, smelling the sweet sticky redness in his glass.

"Well, we're going down to London early tomorrow morning. You should come with us. We can show you around."

Ax swilled the port round his thimble, staring at it intently.

"And don't worry. We'll get you back up," Sivas added.

Ax really wanted to go back to London. And maybe Madinal could be another new friend. That would be two friends in two days. Ax was starting to feel giddy.

"You're right," said Ax. "I'll be there."

"Great," said Sivas as they raised their glasses and the chorus began.

"To the protection and release of humans who were all born to create. I will drink this and commit to sharing my energy and love with them."

Sivas and Ax drained their drinks in one gulp with the other fairies in the dining hall.

"See you out the front at five a.m.," said Sivas.

***

Ax could see two fairies silhouetted in the hazy dawn light. The giant bulb at the front of the building was mimicking the light on Earth.

Sivas's outline was making frequent short, sharp movements. The female fairy's outline was unmoving, with all her weight and one arm placed on one hip.

Sivas caught Ax looking at them out of the corner of his eye. "What are you waiting for? Come on," he said.

Ax quickly flew over. A pillow of perfume lapped around Madinal's body and hit him before he got close.

"Hello," said Ax looking at Madinal who was confidently returning his gaze. "You must be Madinal."

"You're Ax," she said, smiling.

"Yep," he said and gulped.

"I've always wanted to meet you. Son of Maye and grandson of Axone. That must be quite a weight on your shoulders."

"It's normal to me," said Ax.

"Let's go," said Sivas.

"Let's do it," said Madinal, whizzing in a quick loop above the boys.

Ax had never seen Madinal before but The Kingdom's size meant that was quite normal. Especially as Ax did not socialise very much.

"We're taking a direct route to London," said Madinal, lifting herself up and hovering in the air.

"Ax has got to be careful of his energy," Sivas called to Madinal as they descended towards Earth together. "Because of his wing. So, if I say the word, we take him straight back up."

"Got it," said Madinal, looking over at Ax.

Ax could feel himself go red and pressed the back of his hand to his cheek in attempt to cool it down.

Once in Earth's atmosphere they flew over the buzzing streets of London.

"I want you to see the whole array of humans," said Sivas. "You don't get to see much just going up and down to that school of yours."

"Yeah, it's just, it's all my wings can cope with," said Ax. "What's that baby doing on its own in that building?" he asked, suddenly distracted.

"It's being neglected," said Madinal. "It's one of the leading causes of death. And I don't mean their bodies die *physically;* I mean they die *emotionally.* It's as though there is no life in them. Returning a small spark of life to neglected humans is one of the main things that your fairies focus on."

"Your fairies?" asked Ax, puzzled.

"Our fairies. Us fairies," said Madinal.

"Look, that woman is throwing up at the bus stop just like that guy the other day," said Ax.

"They're all so sick. We fairies have a lot of looking after to do," said Sivas.

Ax looked down at a large concrete block to his left and peered in through a single-glazed, lamp-lit window in which he saw a male human on his knees, fingers entwined on his lap, head bowed, rocking back and forth gently. His eyes were closed.

"What's that guy doing?" asked Ax.

"He's asking for help," said Madinal.

"From whom?"

"Us," she said.

"But humans can't see us. They don't know we exist."

"A lot of them know deep *down* that we exist," she explained. "They just refuse to believe in us because they cannot see us. There's a difference."

Ax furrowed his brow.

"It means," Sivas helped out, "that when humans become desperate, they look deep into themselves, remember what they knew at one point in the early stages of human growth – for some this was only in the womb – and call out to us for help, just in case. We always swoop down to save them, look! There's a fairy there going to him now!"

"Oh yes!" said Ax.

It was a beautiful sight. Ax recognised the fairy from The Kingdom. He was glowing golden and flying fast.

The Kingdom fairy dropped down onto the man and delicately tiptoed over his hair. He pulled out a white flannel, lifted it up over the man, and twisted it until oil dripped from the small, soft cloth onto his forehead. The man stopped crying and sat still. Slowly, he dropped his shoulders, breathed deeply, and began to subtly glow the same colour as the fairy from The Kingdom who remained on his head. The glow was fading in and out while the man sat with his eyes closed, no longer rocking.

"Some of them know we're helping," said Sivas. "And some of them ask for help. But others can't see us and that's it. That's where our existence stops for them," he added, pulling his lips into a resigned smile. "Some will never get to know us because they don't dare try it."

Sivas's comment triggered a memory in Ax and, as the three of them continued flying, Ax told them about it.

"When I was a baby fairy my mum told me there was a special bench outside that I could sit on if I needed rest. But when I got outside, I couldn't see any bench," said Ax. "So I just played, ran, and jumped about on the empty, stone-slabbed area. I kept playing until I was too tired to go inside. I hadn't properly learnt the restrictions of my broken wing and I ended up energy-less on the floor, scared and shaking until Mum found me and picked me up."

"Why didn't you sit on the bench?" asked Madinal.

"I couldn't see it."

"But your mum had told you it was there," she said.

"I know," said Ax. "When she picked me up, we went and sat on the bench together. As soon as we sat on it, we felt it. It was invisible but it was there. She put one arm around my shoulder then stroked my hair while I sat on her lap. She said, 'if you had just *tried* to sit on it, you would have found it was here.'."

Ax realised he could empathise with the humans and their need to see the fairies before they would believe in them.

"It's so difficult," said Sivas, "to believe."

"So why don't we just become visible to them? Why are we made unseen?" asked Ax.

Madinal and Sivas both chuckled. "Then we wouldn't be able to do any of our work," said Madinal.

"What?" asked Ax.

"They would just start using us as another tool," said Sivas.

"We need the freedom of being unseen," Madinal added.

"Right," said Ax.

"Don't worry," said Sivas. "Humans have already invented tools to prove the unseen forces of electricity and gravitation. It won't be too long before they will begin to discover what we are, as well."

They found a fence in the shade of a tree on which to rest momentarily. When they set off again Sivas had to help carry Ax. Madinal helped too. The three of them began the journey back up to The Kingdom in comfortable silence.

"Hey, we're just by Marlborough High School," said Sivas. "Do you want to stop and do a quick check on Harper and Jesse before we go back into The Kingdom?"

"I'm quite tired," said Ax. "I'll see them tomorrow."

"But Madinal's never even met them before," said Sivas. Then he had a second thought. "You go back up, I'll show her."

"No, no I'll come with you," said Ax, wanting his new friends to believe he could keep up.

***

"Here we are," said Ax.

The three fairies zoomed up to the window and peered in at the two students who were working before the school day began.

Harper and Jesse were in the science lab which the Headmaster had given them permission to use. A range of documents were spread out over the table in front of them.

On a smaller table to their left were a dozen furry white mice in a clear plastic tub. Next to that lay a few syringes with a pink liquid inside, laid out neatly on a metal tray.

The three fairies flew through the window and hovered next to the shoulders of Harper and Jesse.

Ax broke away and flew closer to the papers. There were drawings everywhere. Pictures of faces. Some of the most beautiful faces he had ever seen. There were doodles of shells, hands, bodies, flowers, and lizard tails.

Over each drawing there was a perfectly straight rectangle design showing their exact proportion. Many had swirls within the rectangles, all of which were divided into thirds.

On the table with the mice and syringes, the fairies could now also see a sign sellotaped to the edge, which read 'divine proportion'.

Then, without warning, a human threw open the lab door and four people trotted into the room. Ax immediately flew up above the table and could see Sivas and Madinal had moved to the top corner of the room by the window.

"What are you up to?" the human girl asked as she strode towards the nearest desk, her high heels clicking hard on the concrete floor.

"We have permission to be in here," said Harper, pushing her glasses up on her nose. "You don't."

The girl looked down at the sign on the table with mice and syringes on. Her tight, dark jeans and skin-hugging vest appeared to be holding her posture up stiff and straight.

"Divine proportion? Are you playing God?" she asked, leaning on her back foot, and looking up at Jesse.

The four humans began to laugh.

"Get out of here," said Jesse.

"Since when did you hang out with geeks, Jesse?" the girl asked.

"I said get out, Tanya," he said, moving an inch closer to her. He looked to his right. "You too, Mark."

"Ooh, okay. She didn't mean to be rude about your girlfriend," said Mark.

Jesse's fists tightened and his jaw clenched as he forced himself not to respond.

"Be careful little boy," said Tanya, flicking her hair behind her shoulder.

Tanya winked at Jesse, let out a little laugh, then turned and walked out with the others close behind her. Mark barely let more than an inch appear between him and Tanya as he jogged out after her.

Ax needed to get out.

He looked around to tell Sivas and Madinal, but they were not in the room. He flew to the window to see if they were there. But his energy had dipped and as he tried to fly up, he just missed the window. He fell to the desk beneath it. His energy was running low.

He waited ten seconds then closed his eyes momentarily in case that helped. He tried flying to the window again.

He couldn't get far enough up.

He tried a third time and, this time, he managed to hold onto the string of the blind then used it to pull himself up.

He saw Sivas and Madinal in the distance.

"Si! Madinal," he called. "Let's go back up."

They turned and looked at him. Madinal just stared. Sivas stared and then caught himself and flew straight over.

"Sorry, are you okay? We got completely distracted. Those humans of yours are pretty odd, huh?"

Ax didn't have the energy to reply. He got into Sivas's arms and they flew up to The Kingdom together.

"Leave me here," said Ax when they arrived at the lobby.

Now that he was back in The Kingdom's atmosphere his energy would increase.

"No worries mate," said Sivas. "See you at dinner and we will plan our next trip."

"Yeah. Sure," said Ax.

Chapter Ten

Harper and Jesse looked at each other as soon as the door clicked shut behind Tanya, Mark, and their two friends.

"Do you know who the other two were?" asked Jesse.

"That's a little beside the point, Jesse," said Harper. "The point is why did they come in here and why have they got an interest in what we do? That was not a coincidence that they found us in here. They knew we were in here." Harper held her pen tightly in her hand.

Jesse's body tensed as he looked at Harper but said nothing. Then he slammed the notebook he had in his hand down on the table and sat in a chair, scraping it on the floor louder that was necessary.

"It's not safe in here," said Harper, marching over to the mice and the syringes. "We're going to have to find another space. We can't use this science lab."

"I haven't told anyone," he said, staring at his laptop screen.

Harper did not respond. She pushed her glasses up on her nose and picked up one of the syringes.

"Let's finish this off," she said, not yet ready to look at Jesse. "We have a free period. We'll carry on working for the next two hours as we were going to, then we'll talk about it after we've eaten lunch."

After a few moments Harper walked over to the table where Jesse was tapping on his laptop. She let her shoulders drop a bit, looked at him, and smiled.

"We need to work fast," she said, "and we clearly need to change where we are doing it. I know you don't tend to take things seriously, Jesse, but this is serious. Uncle Henry has stressed the importance of keeping this a secret for now. We are not just messing with the way people look. If this works, we are affecting the world."

"You don't need to explain how serious it is," he said. "I have no idea why they came in here."

Harper look at him but remained silent, allowing him to continue.

"This is what I want to do," he said. He took a deep breath, the air from the open window refreshing his lungs. "I know the risks. I know the consequences. I want this as much as you do. Uncle Henry is right to want us to help. We are in this together now."

"I know," she said after a beat.

They got back to work. They didn't need to say anything further. The mice they had trialled the injections on had begun reacting exactly as they had predicted. They were now the most beautiful mice they had ever seen, with facial features and bodies in perfect proportion to the golden ratio.

There had, however, been one more change to the mice this morning. They had not been distressed the day before but today they were showing subtle signs of anxiety and of anger, even the most placid mice. They were having to watch the mice's behaviour closely.

The clock carried on ticking while Harper and Jesse carried on working.

The visit from Tanya, Mark, and their pals had been unnerving and now Harper and Jesse were constantly half on the lookout for anyone else approaching. They thought the only person, apart from the Headmaster, who knew they were in there was the science technician and he had no interest in what any of the students did.

"I don't get paid enough to care," he would frequently remind any student or teacher who complained about missing or broken science equipment.

Eventually the bell ran for break and their free period was over. They packed up their papers, put the mice back in the school's state of the art animal testing room, and headed to the canteen.

"I think we should sit separately," Harper said on the walk.

The comment hit Jesse like a whack on the back.

"If you want," said Jesse. "That's no problem."

"Oh, sorry it's not personal," she said. "I just meant I don't want other people to think we're spending time together. It might make them interested in what we're doing."

He understood. It was for obvious practical reasons, but he had become quite attached to Harper. Only a week ago he would not have imagined he would ever *want* to sit with her during break.

"If we were simply doing a science project together," she continued, "we would not suddenly become friends. We haven't spoken for five years and now we spend our time together? It's too weird."

"You're right," said Jesse. "I'm going to spend some time with my friends. I'll insult you probably, and say how boring you are to work with. No offence," Jesse added, "but you really are," he said with a wink.

"None taken," Harper smiled back, shaking her head slightly.

"Hey, guys!" Jesse called after his mates on the other side of the canteen when they arrived.

Harper watched as he jogged to join them, getting instantly tousled in the arm when he got there. They were laughing, chatting and throwing bread rolls in the air as high as they possibly could before catching them. Harper went and sat on her own with her papers hidden firmly in her backpack.

Things were going to be just fine.

Chapter Eleven

Ax sat down for vegetarian spicy rice with Maye and the Elders. It had been a while since they had sat together, and he missed the warm glow of their company. Today's dinner was for a special occasion. Another group of fairies had been born and fairies throughout The Kingdom were singing for their eternal life and health.

The dining hall was filled with smells of cinnamon candles, red roses, and hot baked bread. Sounds of laughter and music tinkled in the background while three or four hundred fairies sang along at a time. The mothers who had recently given birth were at one end of the room and child fairies were taking it in turns to sing over the babies in their arms. The young fairies were excited, as they always were in these amazing atmospheres. They were spinning and twisting in the air, pausing only to move to their seats for a bite to eat, then back up into the air to tumble and laugh and play some more. The room was filled with life and, as it often did during these special times, the floor was gently moving.

Ax noticed Sivas chatting away at a nearby table, but Madinal was nowhere to be seen.

Ax and Sivas exchanged a nod from a distance.

"Is that your friend?" Maye asked following Ax's eye line and looking over at Sivas.

"Not really. Sort of. I guess, yeah," he said.

"I'm glad you're making friends," she said. "I used to worry about you sometimes and feel as though your loneliness was my fault."

"It's not your fault. I was born into this status. And I get to choose what to do with it."

"That's true," said Maye, giving her son a warm smile.

Elba leant over to Ax. "At least you have an excuse to behave recklessly due to the pressures of your role if you ever wanted to," he teased.

"I've been thinking about going back down to Earth a little more often actually," Ax said to Elba, knowing that Maye was listening. It seemed the safest way to broach the subject with her.

"That will be fine, but remember your weaknesses and always listen to your mother," said Elba. "She knows things she hasn't told you yet and only wants what's best for you. You must always remember that, Axone Junior."

"I will," said Ax.

"You know there are some things you still haven't seen," said Elrin, carefully. "We and your mother have been talking about it. We want to take you to see where your grandfather died."

"Oh, really?" asked Ax.

It was rare that his grandfather was mentioned among Maye and the Elders.

"It was in Oxford," added Elson. "We believe we should show you the college library where the battle was fought."

Ax took a deep breath in and a large swig of his sparkling water, spluttering through the ill-paired action. He wiped the drops that fell onto his chest, now deep in thought.

That was why I saw a fairy on top of the flagpole, Ax thought. *That was why I felt at home there. Was— No. That could not have been my grandfather on top of the pole...*

Ax looked up from the wet patch on his chest, adopting an expression as casual as he could muster.

"That would be great," said Ax. "I would really like that. I've never been."

Elson shot a glance at Maye. Ax instantly became anxious.

"Great," said Maye.

"I can't wait," said Ax.

***

"They're going to take me back down to Earth," Ax said to Sivas when they were back in the conservatory by the draigon trees.

Madinal was watering the sweet-smelling basil and fiery rocket, off in her own world, and didn't seem to be listening.

"They're going to show me stuff about my grandfather that I don't yet know," said Ax.

"There's more to your grandfather than we already know?" asked Sivas.

Ax realised that the nature of this conversation was sensitive and that the information the Elders held might be *really* sensitive. He wondered whether, although Sivas was his new friend, he should be talking to him about any of this.

"Yeah, I'm sure it is stuff we know already really," said Ax. "There's no way they could have kept much from me. And besides, if there really were secrets, they would have told me it was confidential. They know that we talk and are friends."

The word friends hung in the air.

"We're friends, yeah. And friends don't keep secrets from each other," said Sivas. "Don't worry, Ax. It will be something perfectly normal."

"What about Madinal?" asked Ax. "I don't necessarily need her to know all this stuff. We're not friends in the same way, if you know what I mean. Can you keep a secret from her, Si?"

Sivas nodded his head with a gentle smile.

"I know exactly what you mean. Don't worry, she's not paying attention to any of this right now and to be honest," Sivas put his hand on Ax's shoulder, "even if you told her straight to her face she probably wouldn't be too interested. She just likes to explore and have fun, you know."

"Yeah, I totally get that," said Ax.

Ax and Sivas looked over at Madinal who really was in her own world, dancing, splattering water onto various fruit trees, occasionally glancing out through the conservatory windows at the infant fairies playing and giggling outside.

"You know I always wanted to ask you what happened in the out-of-bounds room when you were a baby," said Sivas.

They were walking along the glass wall, wiping cobwebs off old fruit baskets that lay lined up on the cold, tiled floor.

Ax looked at Sivas then back at the baskets of various sizes. No one had ever asked him this before.

Ax wanted to tell Sivas what he could remember about being a baby in the out-of-bounds room. But he did not have the information to be generous with. He wanted to build on this new friendship and spill all the secrets he knew: his own secrets, Maye's secrets, the family's secrets. But the truth was he did not have any secrets to tell. There were secrets being kept from *him.*

"I wish I could tell you," said Ax, "but I don't know."

"Yeah, no worries, I thought you might say that. I guess it was so long ago there was a high chance you wouldn't know," said Sivas.

"I'll let you know whatever I find out tomorrow when I'm in Oxford. I'll tell you everything the Elders show me, and I'll report back," said Ax.

"Ah," said Sivas, "I don't know if they'll be happy about that. You telling little me all the new secrets they're about to share with you for the first time?" Sivas shook his head. "Besides, you don't know whether you can trust me, and I'm sure they'll point that out. We've only just met, and they would be right to be suspicious of that. I wouldn't be offended at all. I know how it must look."

"Don't be silly. I can share my personal information with whoever I want. It's the only thing I own. I get to choose who I share that with, no one else does." Ax was looking at

Sivas, the duster hanging distractedly at his side.

"That means a lot," said Sivas.

"Tell you what, why don't you come with me and the Elders tomorrow?" asked Ax.

Sivas looked at him as though he could not be serious.

"I'm serious," Ax continued. "It's just a quick trip to Earth. They would never need to know. You don't have to come *with* us, you could just be there too. Follow behind. They don't even need to see you or speak to you. Not that I'm trying to hide you, it might just make things simpler."

"I think they'd get annoyed," said Sivas, but his face was lighting up excitedly.

"I think you should come. In fact, I'm demanding that you come," said Ax.

"Well, okay. I can't say no to the son of Maye and the grandson of Axone, can I?" Sivas said with a chuckle. "If you're sure?"

"Positive. I insist."

Madinal fluttered over to the two boys, a huge grin on her face.

"What are you two chatting about?" she asked them, wiping a little sweat from her left wing, dazzling the boy fairies with her sparkling hazel eyes.

"We're going on a little adventure tomorrow," said Sivas.

"Ooh, can I come?" she asked.

Ax was about to say no, but before he could Sivas said, "Sure," and Ax did not know what to say.

"Sure," he added more meekly, tugging at the bottom of his t-shirt while Sivas and Madinal got excited about the secret mission with Ax and the Elders to find out about the legendary godfather, Axone.

Chapter Twelve

Elba, Elrin, and Elson met Ax at the side of the building and the four of them got into the fairy car. The Elders were dressed as they always were in baggy brown corduroy trousers, soft brown t-shirts, and, for when it was cooler, brown zip-up fleeces. Fairy cars were hardly ever used and Ax's fingers left their mark in the dust as he opened the door. The Elders were taking extra precautions to get Ax and his damaged wing to Earth and back again safely.

Sivas and Madinal were crouched around the corner, ready to follow Ax. While going through the plan the night before they had reasoned that, even if they were spotted by the Elders, there were so many legitimate reasons to be exploring Oxford that it would not matter. No-one would suspect they were doing anything wrong.

They actually *were not* doing anything wrong and Madinal was reminding Sivas of this.

"We can go wherever we want. We are just hiding to give Ax a bit of privacy and to save the Elders from having to make conversation with his boring friends," she said.

"You're right," said Sivas. "We're doing nothing wrong."

The fairy car started and Elba, Elrin, and Elson began the journey towards Earth with Ax.

Once they were in Earth's atmosphere they slowed down. It was nice for them to spend time together. He usually only saw the Elders when they were with his mum.

Ax knew he must pretend he had never been to Oxford before and so, as they flew over the Radcliffe Camera, Ax tried to look both awestruck and surprised.

"Beautiful, isn't it," said Elson.

"It's a library," added Elba.

The Elders told him many facts about the city and showed no signs of disbelieving that this was his first foray into Oxford.

"There are lots of interesting humans here," Elba said to Ax. "I know you sometimes feel as though you miss out by not having one human with whom you can explore the world, but we want to reassure you that you are encountering most of what other young fairies experience. Besides, what we are showing you today will open a whole new world."

"It's amazing already. Thank you," said Ax.

Ax was beginning to understand why his mum spent so much time with the Elders. They never looked anything special on the outside, just normal, probably boring, very sensible fairies. But he was realising now how serene they were. How calm. How kind. And how deep these traits were embedded within them. He noticed a growing urge to spend a lot more time with them.

"Your mother worries about you," said Elrin. "About you missing out or feeling abnormal."

"I'm fine. You can tell her I'm fine," said Ax. "I've even made some new friends now. Sivas and Madinal."

Ax wondered how far behind the car Sivas and Madinal were. He was pleased they were nowhere to be seen because he was enjoying the private conversation with the Elders.

"There's a lot of intelligence under these roofs, and a lot of hard work accompanying it," said Elson.

"There is also a misconception that intelligence cannot be increased," said Elba.

"Many people believe IQ is static," said Elson. "Or that it can only be moved in small amounts. But that is not true."

Ax had never had conversations like this before. He wanted to listen to what the Elders had to say forever. He sat listening to their slow careful tones. He wanted to absorb it all.

"Ax, we are telling you this because a lot of what your grandfather discovered was to do with intelligence and the way people viewed the world around them. The information he gathered became a threat to some powerful fairies."

There was a moment of silence, then suddenly Ax broke it.

"Did my grandfather get assassinated?" Ax blurted, surprising even himself at what he had just said.

Ax barely realised he was thinking it until he heard himself ask the question.

"No, he didn't get assassinated. He died in battle," said Elrin. "He pushed himself too far. Your mother was there, too."

"Yes, I know," said Ax.

"But," Elrin nodded slowly, "it is fair to say the war would not have happened if your grandfather had not gained certain information."

Ax thought the war had been separate from anything Axone had done. He thought it was just part of a constant battle between Lorkun Lodge and The Kingdom.

"What exactly did he find out?" asked Ax. Talking about his grandfather with the wise Elders was giving him a feeling of electricity crackling through his broken wing.

"We're nearly at the library," said Elson. "We're going to show you."

They continued flying in the car for a moment longer before arriving at the same place Ax had visited with Sivas.

Ax and the Elders entered the building and flew up the red-carpeted stairs and into one of the reading rooms. There were a couple of students listening to music on identical headphones while tapping at identical keyboards on their identical laptops.

"It was in here," said Elba, "that your grandfather found the formula for becoming beautiful, and for seeing beauty in everything."

"And it was in here," added Elrin, "that he was first ambushed and threatened by Vantar's spy."

"What did he get threatened for?" asked Ax.

"They said if any humans discovered what he was doing the whole structure of society would cease to exist and there would no longer be such thing as power or control."

"Right," said Ax, thinking that sounded like a good thing.

"Naturally, your grandfather thought that sounded like a good thing," said Elba.

Ax smiled.

"The problem was the Lorkun fairies did not agree," Elba continued.

"They found out something else," added Elson. "Something Axone never even told your mother."

"What was that?" Ax asked.

"We can't tell you. Not in here. There may be fairies listening."

Ax thought about Sivas and Madinal and wondered whether they were close enough to be eavesdropping. He did not dare look around for them. If Sivas and Madinal were here, then he did not want to know about it at this moment.

"We'll be able to talk safely on the library roof, and you will see the pole your grandfather fell off when the battle was coming to an end. The night he–"

Ax smiled with a small nod to show Elrin it was okay to say it.

"–the night he died," Elrin finished.

Ax's brain was fizzing.

"This way," Elson said as he flew off.

He led the way up to the top left corner of the room above the window and pushed a tattered encyclopaedia to the side. A hole was revealed and one by one they crept through.

The four of them stood on top of the roof, the strong, cold winds making it difficult for them to retain their balance. The wind, however, also ensured it was too noisy for anyone else to hear what they had to say.

Ax's gaze remained on the pole. He tried to conjure up the image that had come into his mind last time he was here. But he could not recreate the picture of what he now knew were his grandfather's last moments alive.

"This is where your grandfather fell off," said Elba, pointing to the top of the pole as his eyes began to well up.

Elrin kindly took over. "And that dining hall is where your mother carried him. Your grandfather lay in her arms while she told him he would get better and made plans to get him back up to The Kingdom."

Elba smiled at Elrin.

"She had you in her womb and cradled your grandfather while he died. Your mother said hope sparkled in his eyes right until the moment he left this world."

"Ax, your grandfather never told Maye about this formula that would make people see the world with new, profound equality," said Elson. "Axone did not tell anyone that the effect of being equally beautiful would also cause people to consider themselves equal in all other ways – intellect being one. When they feel beautiful, they feel *good*, and while they vibrate a good feeling, they attract things that are currently reserved for a select few: money, love, and power."

"She only found out later, through us, about the secret world your grandfather had been creating, why he had been in danger, and why the humans seeing beauty everywhere would destroy hierarchical structures," added Elba. "No other fairies in The Kingdom knew about the true reason behind the wars."

"Do you mean, if The Kingdom and Lorkun Lodge fought another war now, it would still be about beauty?" Ax asked, listening intently, desperately trying to absorb all this new information.

"Yes. If a battle was fought again now, Lorkun Lodge will begin it, and it would still be about beauty and how it affects human society."

"But Mum knows now?" asked Ax.

"Yes," said Elrin.

"Ax, you must never, ever tell this to anyone," said Elba.

"I promise."

"If Lorkun Lodge attacks again, and many Elders across all fairy lands believe they are going to, and if The Kingdom doesn't win, then the chemical to make humans beautiful will be destroyed. If that happens, the humans will never know true freedom from the way they look. Vantar will become the ruler of all fairy lands, and he will be able to infiltrate The Kingdom and erase what fairies already know."

Ax's heart felt as though it was becoming cold. He continued listening.

"The humans will forever be trapped by possessions, products, and a perpetual drive to be considered beautiful in some way," explained Elba. "They will no longer know how to let go. All our work will be undone."

"And if we do win?" asked Ax.

"The chemical would be administered to the humans and true freedom from the material world, from possessions, and from perceptions of their own beauty, would be achieved," said Elrin.

"Do you know when there might be another battle?" asked Ax.

"Your mother wanted to tell you herself, but it was not safe for her to be down here with you because the threats from the Lorkun Lodge have been arriving with more frequency into the out-of-bounds room. They may be preparing to attack at any moment," said Elson.

"We believe they may have found where the formula is or at least have an inkling where it went to," said Elba.

"If they find it, they will declare war with the sole aim of destroying it," continued Elson.

"And if they don't find the formula?" asked Ax.

"They won't start a battle until they have located it. It is too risky if they can't guarantee the formula is gone," Elson explained.

Ax breathed in deeply then pushed his shoulders down as he released the breath. He looked out over Oxford from the roof of the college library while the lights sparkled in the night. It was such a lot of information to take in.

Then Ax remembered Harper and Jesse and what he had heard them say about the chemical they were working on. That couldn't possibly be what they were working on. Could it?

He stood up straight and took a panicked deep quick breath in. His eyes were wide, and he looked straight ahead. He did not dare look at the Elders. He had to get to Harper and Jesse and let them know how much was at stake. If, of course, that was what they were working on.

"I need to go back," Ax said to the Elders, sharply, still looking straight in front of him.

"I know it's a lot to take in," said Elrin.

Ax turned around and started walking. "I need to go back. I need to go back now."

The Elders looked at each other.

"I am sorry to have told you all this," said Elson. "We didn't want to unless we really had to. But the threat is real, and we had to let you know. But for now, we will take you home."

Ax said nothing.

They were sitting on the cracked leather seats of the car, travelling back up to The Kingdom in silence except for the chugging and gargling of the engine. Then it hit him. Sivas and Madinal. Where were they? Where had they been when the Elders told him what was going on?

Chapter Thirteen

Harper passed Jesse the key which the school's scruffy-haired and perpetually moody caretaker had given them hours earlier.

He had handed them to Harper saying, "I don't care what you need the hut for as long as you clear it up afterwards. Goodness knows why the Headmaster wanted to let you use this space."

Jesse turned the long heavy key. They listened to the solid metal bar slide against the back of the wooden door and clunk into a new position. They looked at each other and smiled. Jesse pushed the unlocked door.

A tuft of dust blew across the wooden floor as a breeze entered the room. Fragments of Autumn sun were scattered over the large wooden table that sat in the middle of the square room.

They walked in, and up to the table. Jesse tapped his fingers on the sticky surface.

"It might need a little clean-up," he said, looking at the blackness that had appeared on his fingertips. "We could totally have a proper mad party in here," he added, turning to look at Harper with his eyebrows raised and massive grin on his face.

Harper rolled her eyes. She walked over to the sink in the right-hand corner of the room, behind which was a large cracked mirror and a few pieces of crockery. The smell of mildew from the damp sink and the cracks in the windowsill said the room had not been used for a while.

"It's perfect," Harper announced, turning from the sink to look at Jesse. "We'll bring our laptops and cleaning products tomorrow. It won't take much."

"I'll bring a cafetiere and a football," he replied. "I can practice kick-ups here," he said stepping into the open space to the left of the table and thrusting his knees up with an invisible ball.

***

Six weeks later…

It was the beginning of November. The shabby hut now smelt of sea-breeze cleaning spray, pizza, and filter coffee. With the help of Uncle Henry, Harper and Jesse had finally managed to convince their parents to let them spend evenings and weekends in the hut. Uncle Henry had phoned the Headmaster who duly wrote their parents a letter explaining that he was happy for the students to use the school's space for something so interesting and beneficial to the future of their academic career.

Jesse's parents read the letter and barely batted their eyelids. He was still unsure whether his dad had actually read it. He had handed the letter back to Jesse, barely looking away from his iPad as he did so, with a "sure son, whatever you want". His mum had put up a bit more of a fuss but he could smell the alcohol fumes coming from her while she protested, and there was always a chance she would not remember anything about it next morning when she woke up.

Harper's parents had kicked up more of a fuss but calmed down when they received the letter from the Headmaster. Still, her mum was texting her multiple times a day, suggesting she would be better off working at home.

Harper and Jesse were planning the event that would formally launch their product. They had put together posters to advertise the launch. Jesse had been in charge of researching how to make an advert compelling and Harper had been in charge of doing the maths to work out the ticket prices.

Harper and Jesse were barely sleeping. Their current routine was: go to the hut straight after school, work all evening with a pot noodle, or a thin-based pizza, go home to sleep at one a.m., get back up at five a.m. before the sun rose, go to the hut, then work with steamy coffee (which Harper had been learning to drink in place of her usual sweet milky tea) and eat two slices of toast and jam each while working before school. If either of them yawned or rubbed their eyes, the other would pretend not to have noticed. They knew they were in this game together and their best chance of survival was ignoring signs of tiredness in themselves and in each other.

They were advertising the event as an artistic beauty convention, with emphasis on the arts to attract a wider audience than just the typical beauty community. The convention would have something for a wide range of artistic interests to sell as many tickets as possible. There would be models, actors, comedians, painters, and dancers at the event. The day would include free lessons on how to draw, how to apply make-up, how to style an outfit, and more. The theme throughout would be beauty, and the angle would be a mathematical perspective on beauty in the natural world.

All the lessons would implement the golden ratio which they would be labelling 'divine proportion' as they both agreed it was a more exciting term. Harper had found a huge warehouse in South London to use for the event and Jesse was beginning the floor plan for the day, sketching out where to put the stalls, the main stage, and the backstage area.

The tickets were expensive but there would be freebies. That was Harper's idea. The itinerary was still being tweaked but one thing they were sure on was that the day would end with one big talk delivered by Harper and Jesse during which they would, finally, demonstrate the use of the injection.

Harper had broached the subject of how, and indeed when, the injections would be administered.

"Do we sign people up for the injection which they can use another day? Or, do we say the injection is ready to go and do live demonstrations on real people?" asked Harper.

"If we do it there and then, there's no room for people to change their minds," Jesse considered. "But the backlash and potential for it to go wrong is then huge."

This same conversation went back and forth every time they had a moment to sit quietly, sometimes during pizza eating, sometimes during a lull in the early morning in which they sipped coffee.

"We want to give everyone time to book the injection, pay for it, and think about what they are doing," said Harper.

"But equally, if everyone is sufficiently wowed during the day, then the atmosphere will be perfect for getting people to sign up on the spot without time to think about consequences, worry about the price, or simply forget how gorgeous everything they saw was on the day," said Jesse.

Harper sighed.

"We're going to have to decide soon," Jesse said taking a sip of Italian roast and tipping back in his chair. The sunlight shining through the window threw a warm beam over the right side of his chest.

"I know," said Harper. She too had a coffee in her hand but was looking down, tapping her pen on the table. She pushed her glasses up on her nose and looked at Jesse.

"Man, I miss partying," said Jesse. "It's going to feel so good when this is over," he added. "No offence," he said looking at Harper with a smile.

She understood. Their lives had become very different in the past two months.

Jesse put his hands through his hair and shook his head slightly as if to shake off a thought. He walked over to the mice. They were still perfectly beautiful and, although they had become a little rowdy at one point, and then quite stressed and anxious, this phase did not last long, and they had completely calmed down in the end. Harper and Jesse were receiving frequent deliveries and detailed instructions from Uncle Henry and the final product was nearly ready to try. Fascinatingly the mice re-created their original power hierarchy and societal structure after only a couple of days. They rearranged themselves into the original groups with only one or two going back to a very slightly different position than before.

"What if the humans don't replicate this pattern?" asked Jesse.

Harper didn't say anything but pulled her phone out and began a video call to Uncle Henry.

She walked over to Jesse, phone in hand, and sat next to him, the phone now held up in front of both their faces.

"Hi!" said Uncle Henry as his face popped into the screen.

"We have a question," said Harper.

"It's more of a general and growing concern," said Jesse.

"Fire away!" said Uncle Henry, leaning back on a bean bag on his balcony in the hills of Los Angeles.

"How close is the behaviour of humans to the behaviour of animals?" asked Jesse.

"The behaviour of humans is different to animals in one key way," said Uncle Henry, one arm now behind his head, propping himself up a little further. "Animals do what they were made to do without question. Bees make honey. Moles dig holes. They do not have an option to stop. Humans are wired to create, but here's the difference. Humans can now opt out of writing, drawing, singing, building, cooking, or dancing if they want to." He reached down and found a drink on the floor. He lifted it up and took a long sip through a straw.

"How important is that going to be?" asked Harper.

"Mojito mocktail," said Uncle Henry, putting the drink back on the floor. "Important? It's all important. But *exciting*? That is what makes the whole thing very exciting. The potential to take this in directions we are unable to yet imagine is what makes the injection exciting."

"Right," said Jesse, wondering whether terrifying, dangerous, or stupid might be better words than exciting.

"Thanks, Uncle Henry," said Harper.

"Other than that concern is everything okay?" he asked.

"Yes, really good," said Harper.

"Great, well I'll phone you again soon. There's really nothing to worry about," said Uncle Henry. "I've been working on this for seventeen years. The time is perfect and you're the right people to help with it."

"Okay," said Harper.

They said goodbye and hung up.

"I always feel better after talking to him," said Jesse.

"Same," said Harper. "I don't know why my mum thinks he's so bananas. He's great."

Harper and Jesse had received the necessary clearing to use the formula on humans from the medical lab via an ecstatic email from Uncle Henry the next morning. Uncle Henry was due in the country at the end of December and would be at the event which had been scheduled to coincide with his trip.

Harper was looking forward to seeing him again and Jesse was looking forward to meeting him for the first time.

***

Five weeks later…

School had shut for the holidays and Harper and Jesse were working as hard as before. They had become militantly strict with their diet now, too. They realised they could not risk a sugar crash. They ditched the toast with jam and the pot noodles. They were eating healthily and drinking a lot more water.

There were now three electric heaters in the room which, even when on full blast, often felt futile against the cold winds and thin walls. There was also now an old printer on the floor at the side of the room which they had used to print out their flyers for the event in the early days of the planning. They had since ramped up the promotion online and the advertising company's statistics told them they had reached over ninety thousand people with their online advertisements.

The day had finally arrived for the initial release of tickets which were due to go on sale at midnight. Harper and Jesse were having last minute doubts about whether anyone would actually want to buy one.

It was five minutes to midnight and the web link was about to go live.

Harper and Jesse sat side-by-side with Jesse's laptop in front of them. Jesse was wearing the same pair of jeans he had been wearing for a week, but he had been home to put on a clean t-shirt. His parents had been surprised to see him. Harper was also wearing jeans. Her t-shirt was white, and her hair was long and silky, although distinctly unclean.

"Only a few minutes left," said Harper, looking at the laptop screen.

Jesse clicked onto the webpage.

He looked at Harper. "This is it," he said.

She smiled and pushed her glasses up on her nose. "What if we don't sell a single one?" she asked.

They both laughed.

"It's not that unlikely," said Jesse. "We haven't really known what we've been doing."

Jesse started jiggling his knee up and down while Harper sat upright looking at the screen, her hands in her lap.

The clock turned midnight.

Jesse refreshed the page.

"What's going on?" he asked.

Harper leant closer and Jesse clicked refresh a couple more times. It was broken.

"Shit," he said. "What's happened? Why isn't it working?"

"Don't worry," said Harper but her face gave away the disappointment she felt.

"What's happened? I think the computer's crashed?"

"We probably should have tested the link first," said Harper starting to stand up. "It doesn't matter at all. We'll just send an email and try again tomorrow."

"No, we need to get this sorted as soon as possible," said Jesse.

Harper walked over to the sink to grab a glass of water.

"This is a disaster," Jesse carried on. He raised his voice slightly so Harper could still hear while at the sink. "If we can't even get the first link up what does that say to the world about our competency. We're trying to get them to hand over money to a brand they've never heard of for a product they've never tried. And we can't even get a link to work. We need to get this sorted quick before anyone sees this. This is a mess."

Harper walked back over to the desk. She began fiddling away, checking, and rechecking the URL of the site on her laptop. The hyperlink was written correctly.

"Why can't we get onto the page?" Harper asked as though Jesse had not been saying that repeatedly for the past minute. "Log on again?" she suggested.

"I'm logging on again and again," he said. "Ah! It worked!"

Harper stood behind Jesse to look at his laptop screen.

"Thank goodness for that," she said, leaning forward over Jesse's shoulder.

They both stared at what was on the screen.

"Sold out."

It was impossible. It could not be possible. It had only been live for a couple of minutes and there had been two thousand tickets up for sale.

They refreshed the page. It said it again.

"Sold out."

Jesse logged onto his emails with Harper still standing behind him not daring to look away from the screen.

There was a new email in his inbox from EventSellers.

"Congratulations," it read. "Your event has sold out."

Jesse kept his left hand on the keypad and his right hand motionless on the desk.

They had sold two thousand tickets in under three minutes.

They looked at each other and started to laugh.

"We did it. We did it!"

They stood up, they hugged, they jumped up and down.

"We actually did it," said Jesse.

"Beauty," said Harper under her breath, now standing still.

"They want to come," said Jesse, more to himself than to Harper, now also standing still.

"We just made…" Harper thought for a moment doing the maths in her head. "Five hundred thousand pounds."

They stood still, frozen at the unbelievable sum, then burst out laughing again.

"We're rich," said Jesse.

"This is it," added Harper.

"This is just the beginning," said Jesse. "We need to get some beers to celebrate."

"We've got an event to finish planning," Harper pointed out.

"Right, yeah, true," said Jesse who had not drunk alcohol in over a month and was surprised at how fine he felt about it.

They began working on the rest of the details. The adrenaline was now surging, and they happily continued working at the desk despite the lateness of the hour. Jesse made them coffee. They sent an email out to everyone who bought a ticket to thank them for purchasing it and to send them the final details about the event.

There were floods of messages on the event page from people who were furious they could not get a ticket.

'It had crashed. FFS'

'Set my alarm for midnight and it had already sold out by the time I logged on.'

'Anybody want to sell me their ticket? Willing to pay more than original price.'

Harper and Jesse decided to go home with the aim of getting some proper sleep. They were also going to need more supplies for the hut.

If the public reaction was anything to go by, this was about to be ramped up and the work hours were going to get even more insane.

"Good luck sleeping," Jesse said as they parted.

"Yeah, I mean, I won't," said Harper with a huge smile on her face. "There is so much adrenaline in my body right now."

"I know exactly what you mean," said Jesse.

They were at home trying to sleep and began texting each other until the early hours of the morning with suggestions and details they needed to write down and work out when they were back in the hut together. Goody bags should be created. The colours needed deciding. The timings. The free tea and coffee. The snack room. The toilet roll. The music. The lighting. The pen colour and the branding on the outside. It would be slightly festive as it was so close to Christmas. They thought about the social media tags and hashtags and adverts and platforms. The secrecy with which they would detail the directions to the event would be used to build up even more anticipation. They would keep emails and instructions to the guests cryptic, just for fun. The more secretive Harper and Jesse made the information, the more the intrigue was built around it. This was going to be a big event and if Harper and Jesse played their cards right it looked as though they were headed for the big time.

The next day Harper and Jesse were ready to start deflecting phone calls from the press. The event was being talked about all over social media.

"Did you sleep?" Jesse asked Harper as she walked up the path to the hut in the morning with wet hair.

"No," she said with a smile.

They went in and sat down and put ground coffee into the cafetiere before filling it with boiling water. The emails were unrelenting. Some were asking questions about aspects of the event. Most were simply trying to blag a ticket.

All requests were shut down with a "Sorry, we are sold out," from Harper and Jesse, no matter which media outlet the request was coming from. Every appeal for an interview was turned down politely by Harper and Jesse. This was not time for distractions. This was time to get serious.

They wrote and planned and edited and practised the talk and emailed it back and forth to Uncle Henry. The talk would be delivered at the end of the event, the most important part of the day.

Chapter Fourteen

Ax flew into a large room in the Elder's wing of The Kingdom. It was hardly ever used and Ax was pleased to find the room empty. He sat on the door handle, his back against the door, and breathed in and out slowly. He had been feeling anxious ever since his trip to the college in Oxford with the Elders.

He straightened up, shook off his momentary stress, and flew over to the big mahogany desk at the window. He opened the drawer beneath it with the swirly metal key that sat in the lock. He picked up a pen, a pot of black ink, and a sheet of paper from within the drawer. He lay the sheet of thick parchment on the table and dipped the pen in the ink.

Then he started drawing the design. Over and over on the sheet. The design he had seen across all of Harper and Jesse's papers in the school. He drew the swirl and he drew the rectangles that had a mathematic formula, guaranteed to create beauty no matter what culture or time you lived in, or so their notes claimed.

He drew it five times. *How am I going to use this to get the message to Jesse and Harper,* he wondered. *They can't see me.*

Many weeks had passed since Ax had found out the true extent of what Harper and Jesse may have their hands on, and he was no closer to working it out.

He had never had to communicate with a human before. Many fairies had never explicitly communicated with them. Fairies would often connect through a jolt of encouragement, or nudges of laughter and joy, but rarely a specific warning or obvious sign was needed to force a human to do something.

Ax carried on looking at the drawings in front of him.

Maybe Sivas will help me, he thought.

He had not seen Sivas or Madinal since his visit to Oxford with the Elders. Where were they? What had they heard on that trip? Were they nearby at all? He needed to speak to them. Sivas would help him work out what to do.

Just at that moment Sivas appeared at the window. Ax opened it and let him in.

"How did you know I was here?" Ax asked. "And that I was thinking about you?" he added.

"One of the Elders said he saw you come this way," said Sivas. "You were thinking about me?"

"Yes. Were you there? In Oxford? Did you hear the conversation on the roof? About my grandfather?" Ax asked.

"No. Madinal and I could see you, but we were on the roof of the dining hall and it was too windy to make out what you were saying. We could barely hear each other let alone your voices all the way over on the library roof."

"Okay, okay, I'll fill you in," said Ax, trying to breathe calmly.

Sivas went to the mantelpiece and filled two glasses with the teenage favourite, a Bloody Mary. They said cheers, thanked the humans for yet another delicacy that had been created in The Kingdom, then sipped the drinks.

"Gosh these are good," said Sivas.

"Yeah," said Ax, taking another swig, wondering how Sivas appeared to be totally chilled.

"I've never been in one of these rooms before. They're swish," said Sivas.

"Yeah," said Ax. He took another sip.

"So, what did they say? What's the deal?" asked Sivas.

"Well," said Ax, "Harper and Jesse have something that my grandfather lost a while ago. I don't know how they got hold of it or whether they know its full effects. There was no way of knowing what it was unless someone did tests on it. Well, it seems now that they have."

"Right," said Sivas, listening intently.

"It can be very dangerous to humans. Harper and Jesse probably don't know this, or at least the full extent of it, but if it is to be used, and if Lorkun Lodge finds out who's using it, war will almost certainly be restarted among the fairy lands, and this time it will not end until someone has won. Not if the humans are this close to administering the injection."

Ax took a sip of his drink and turned back to look at Sivas who was deep in thought.

Ax considered whether he should tell Sivas the rest. That it could mean destruction for the whole human structure if they *do* take it, but no freedom for the whole human race if they *don't* take it.

"Gosh," said Sivas. "Well, I think we should tell Madinal. She will be able to help on this one."

Ax was instantly glad he had not said too much and decided not to say anything further. Sivas had enough information to help.

"I don't really know Madinal," said Ax. "I would rather just keep this between me and you."

"Don't worry, you can trust her. She's my friend and a friend of mine is a friend of yours. You're my friend, Ax."

Ax could not help feeling flattered.

"Yeah, I trust you," said Ax. "We need to get down to the school and warn them. We need to somehow ruin the chemical they are going to use. We need to make sure the Lorkun fairies believe that it is a dud."

"When are we going?" asked Sivas.

"As soon as possible," said Ax.

Chapter Fifteen

Although their names were not on the invites, a rumour had immediately spread around Marlborough High that it was Harper and Jesse's secret project as soon as the tickets had gone live.

At first the Headmaster had not been pleased about it being plastered all over social media. He called Harper and Jesse to his office for a meeting during which he painstakingly went through the pros and cons with them while they ate a plate of custard creams and drank milky tea. Well, the Headmaster went through all the cons, then Harper and Jesse went through all the pros. The Headmaster didn't mention the fact that he knew Uncle Henry.

"I guess you kids are unstoppable then," he said towards the end of the meeting.

The custard cream with a broken corner was now alone on the plate between them, accompanied by only a few crumbs, and the bottoms of all three mugs were now visible.

"Well, yes," said Jesse.

Both him and Harper knew they needed the Headmaster onside. They wanted him to trust them with their promotion. Uncle Henry was pleased with the press coverage. But the Headmaster seemed more nervous. It was the first time Harper and Jesse had properly sat down to talk to him. They noticed the deep lines over his face which reflected the amount of time he had dedicated to students who were falling by the wayside, and his thin frame which showed he was still too busy dealing with the students to regularly sit and eat.

Eventually the three of them came to an agreement. Harper and Jesse would continue to use Marlborough High's hut and remain in control of the promotion. In return, the school would be advertised along with the injection, and would be represented positively at the event.

The more Harper and Jesse turned down interview offers the more people became desperate to know about them. Over the coming days, the press had no interviews with Harper and Jesse to print. They had no official photographs of Harper and Jesse to publish. They had no comment from the Headmaster or Harper and Jesse's parents to make an article out of. Instead, they began printing photos of the outside of the run-down, shabby building in which they were working, accompanied by around a thousand words on what they imagined the inside to look like, usually with a few utterly bizarre quotations from fellow students scattered throughout the piece.

Harper and Jesse would sometimes sit and read an article together for a laugh. They also rather enjoyed reading the speculation as to what ingredients were included in the injection. They even spent one dinner eating vegan sausages and sweet potato mash while reading the suspected effects and components of the formula.

None of the published suggestions got close to the truth. A form of acid was the most common guess, and one newspaper assured their readers that the injection would make you beautiful for a while but then would make your face collapse "from the outside in".

"Incredible," said Harper trying to keep the mash in her mouth while she laughed.

"Hmmm, I know, 'the outside in'!" Jesse mocked, tapping his pen on the side of his forehead, doing an impression of a journalist trying to come up with an original way of saying 'inside out' to impress his editor and their readership. "Oh, I know it doesn't mean the same thing, but they won't notice!"

Jesse and Harper had become good at making each other laugh.

There was one thing on which they were concentrating most amidst the madness that surrounded them, and that was the actual drug.

A lot of hype and excitement had built up around them but within the walls of the rundown hut Harper and Jesse were working harder than ever and were feeling the pressure despite Uncle Henry's reassurance.

They were confident with all the trials and tests now, and Uncle Henry was emailing them multiple times a day to pass on more information about the injections, but there was one topic they never liked to broach: what if the drug destroyed the structure of human society to the point of no return?

What if the power they were given, to achieve actual freedom, was destructive rather than liberating as they had previously assumed?

Uncle Henry said it was the best thing that could happen. But Harper and Jesse knew they both frequently worried about it. Once, when the disintegration of power was mentioned in a widely shared, ten-thousand-word piece online, closely reflecting the truth about what Harper and Jesse had seen in the mice, they sat in silence for five minutes.

They were unable to explain how the press knew that, then got back to work, palpably more nervous than before.

They agreed that they would do *one* press conference on the event day. There was now less than a week until the sold-out event. They would do the press conference at the end of the day. They had decided it would be better to do it after the main attraction, when they could be totally open about the success of the event without giving any spoilers to those that had paid for the event. Neither of them wanted to admit that they were concerned about doing it after in case something on the day went wrong, in which case talking to the press would be the last thing they would want to do.

Chapter Sixteen

Maye and the Elders were in the out-of-bounds room. The walls of the room were made of fairy spirit and, therefore, were not painted but glowed a warm gold the whole time. A fresh smell of white lilies on the mantelpiece filled the room.

Maye curled up into the soft armchair next to the invention that showed everything that happened in the fairy atmosphere and on Earth. The TV resembled an Earthly TV just in case anyone happened to see it. It was always on, but usually on mute, and it was the reason the out-of-bounds room remained out of bounds.

Nobody except Maye and the Elders knew about the TV and its capabilities. Using it, it was possible to zoom in on any area, at any time, in The Kingdom or on Earth, and hear and see what was happening.

"We need to think really hard about this. But we need to see what's going on," said Maye.

"It's up to you," said Elba, bringing sparkling water over to Maye in her chair. "But you know once you have seen it you cannot unsee what other people are up to, and sometimes it's healthier to not know."

"Yes," said Maye. "I have tried many times to forget some of the things that I know."

"Ax is going to be okay," said Elba.

"We all know that's not true," said Maye.

She took a sip of her bubbly drink then placed it on a coaster on the small table next to the chair.

"Where is he now?" asked Elrin.

"Down on Earth with that Sivas fairy," said Maye. "And to think all these years I had wanted him to make a friend. Why did it have to be that one?"

"You could have banned it," said Elson.

"I will not ban my son from doing anything he wants. I can merely watch him and sing love for him. His choices must be his own."

Maye sat up straighter and stretched her arms, then got out of the armchair and began flying up and down the room while the Elders sipped their drinks.

"Will you remind me of his reaction during the college tour?" Maye asked.

"He didn't take the news too well," said Elson, lifting his glass to his mouth and raising his eyebrows.

"But it was news to him at least. Which means he did not know as much as we thought," said Elrin.

"He flew off as soon as we got home," added Elson, "and didn't say a thing on the journey back."

Maye flew back to the table next to her armchair and took another sip of her drink. "And does he know we are watching him now or that we *can* watch him?"

"He did a pretty good job of pretending he had never been to Oxford before, so no. I don't think he does."

"Okay," said Maye. "And you said he's with Sivas now?"

"Yes. Down towards the school with Sivas and Madinal. We don't know who Madinal is."

"Do you think she is a threat?" asked Maye.

"We don't know."

"Have we received any more threats from Lorkun Lodge?" she asked.

"They are continuing," said Elson.

The Elders looked at each other and then at Maye who was staring at them in anticipation.

"They are becoming more frequent," said Elrin.

"Right," said Maye. "How frequent?"

"They've gone from one a week, to one—" Elba started then paused.

172

"–everyday," Elrin finished off.

Maye flew to the TV and absentmindedly brushed some of the dust off the screen with her fingers. She turned to look at the Elders.

"And do you think they know where the formula is?" she asked.

"No," said Elba. "They still don't know that, and they will not do anything until they do. They think they are getting closer but cannot confirm exactly where yet. They will be working fast though, and I think they currently have an idea."

"Should we let Ax carry on?" asked Maye.

"Only you can make that decision," said Elson.

"I know," said Maye.

"You have never interfered with his destiny before," said Elson. "You always said nature must take its course. Even knowing what you know."

"The one saving grace of what I know is that it always seemed in the distant future. Not anymore." Maye's voice went quiet and she looked down. "I don't know if I can lose a father and a son."

There was a moment of silence while Maye stood by the TV with her eyes closed. When she was ready, she opened them and sat back in the armchair.

"Well, I want to keep a close eye on him at the moment," said Maye.

"Of course," Elrin assured her.

"And I want you to show me everything. Even if he is in danger. *Especially* if he is in danger. But we do not go and help," Maye looked at the Elders, "unless we have my word. You will leave him and history and fate alone unless I," her voice nearly cracked, but she composed herself, "unless I, and only I, say that we can intervene."

"We will only ever act on your word," said Elson.

"You're the only one who can make the decision," confirmed Elba.

Elrin smiled with a nod.

Maye reached for her drink and spun the straw round, hitting the ice against the glass while she struggled to take in the gravity of what she was deciding. She heard the Elders take small sips of their drinks but remained looking at her own glass. She always knew she would let nature take its course with her son. She was in charge of The Kingdom, but believed she had no right to interfere with destiny, even if the power to make that decision had been put in her hands. She felt relieved to have given herself the caveat in her speech just now. She had a get out clause. If it got too much. If she wanted to. If she said so. They would intervene.

"Remember when Ax was just a baby in here," Elba said to Maye, breaking the silence.

Maye looked up.

"Yes," she smiled. "Back to where all this began. I chose to keep his wing as it was, knowing what it meant. Knowing what it meant to his grandfather. Knowing what it meant to the destiny of The Kingdom and the humans below. My son."

The Elders left the out-of-bounds room. Maye remained and sang a sweet song to herself of peace.

Chapter Seventeen

Sivas, Ax, and Madinal were nearly at the school. Sivas had finished giving Madinal all the details on the journey down. Ax had felt uncomfortable at moments hearing the information being relayed in someone else's words, but he trusted Sivas and, besides, he needed their help.

Sivas and Madinal had not travelled in a fairy car before, but they were using one today, just in case. They decided that Ax would give the signal of three slow, large movements of his good wing if he felt his energy become low, at which point they would help him back into the fairy atmosphere where he could regain energy.

"Good for you for not telling the Elders about Harper and Jesse," said Madinal just as they were approaching Marlborough High.

"While I was in Oxford?" asked Ax.

"Exactly. Good that you kept your humans safe. The Elders clearly wouldn't understand what the students were up to or know how to deal with it."

"Yeah," said Ax.

Ax had in fact been contemplating telling the Elders about Harper and Jesse. He thought they would be able to help and that they would understand. Not his mother, she did not need to know. She would only worry about him. But the Elders would help him, and they'd know what to do. It had not crossed his mind that they might be, as Madinal said, untrustworthy and not have Harper and Jesse's best interests in mind. From what he knew fairies always prioritised humans' needs. Especially once they were given their own human to look after and so knew what that responsibility felt like. But then, the Elders did not have one human they were responsible for. Maybe Madinal was right.

They landed on the roof of the run-down building in which Harper and Jesse were working.

"Goodness me, could this have any more holes in it?" asked Madinal, fluttering on the cracked tiles scattered over the roof of the hut. "They won't cope with this if it gets much colder."

"I think they have heaters inside," said Sivas.

The three of them flew in and had a look around the room. They flew over the heads of Harper and Jesse for a bit, then Sivas and Madinal explored the room.

Ax stayed with Harper and Jesse. They were talking about the logistics of the press conference they were going to do and what would be most appropriate to wear.

Ax, Sivas, and Madinal then settled on the main table in the middle of the room. It was covered in plans and blueprints and formulas and sums.

Ax found the formula first.

"This is the chemical compound that is wanted by the Lorkun fairies," Ax called to Sivas and Madinal.

They immediately flew over.

"How are we going to destroy this before any of the Lorkun fairies find it?" asked Ax.

"How do we know they don't already know about this?" asked Sivas.

"Harper and Jesse have not been letting humans in here," said Ax, "so it's unlikely they will have gained much attention from Lorkun fairies. If that's the case, Lorkun Lodge may not know about this until the day the project is launched."

"Well that's good," said Sivas.

Madinal was studying the formula.

"It is. It really is," she muttered.

"We could spill ink on it," suggested Sivas.

"Yeah, that doesn't solve the problem that a batch of the product is probably already made and ready to go," said Ax.

"Yeah, sorry. Silly idea," said Sivas.

While the fairies were discussing it, Jesse picked up the sheet of A4 from under the fairies and they all fell onto the table.

He walked over and showed it to Harper. Sivas began flying around the room looking for the syringes. Their next plan was to destroy the doses that had already been created. The humans would be able to make more, but not in time for the event, so the fairies would buy themselves some time.

Jesse had put the paper back onto the table and Madinal was standing on it again.

Sivas beckoned Ax over to a metal filing cabinet.

"I think the syringes might be in here. It's the only place I haven't looked. But I can't get it open," said Sivas.

Ax had a look at the cabinet which had a large dent on the side and looked as though it had been a student's locker. Ax pulled hard at the padlock. Fairies were unusually strong for their size, but it did not budge.

"How are we going to get in?" asked Ax.

Sivas gave the lock a pull, but the locker just moved a little more while the padlock remained firmly shut.

There was a knock at the door of the hut. The fairies stayed still but Jesse immediately started turning papers face down on the table while Harper slowly tip-toed toward the door.

"Just a minute!" she called.

Before opening the door, she peered through the small peephole which magnified everything on the outside. It was someone she hadn't seen before.

Harper turned around, looked at Jesse, and shrugged her shoulders.

It was probably a journalist.

Jesse shrugged back.

"I'm sorry, we're in the middle of something," called Harper. "Can you email us instead? We can't open up at the moment."

The person who had knocked started muttering and wandered off. Although Marlborough High had put up barbed wire and a new, improved lock on the gate since the press coverage had become intense, some of the journalists were still managing to get through.

"How do they keep getting in?" Harper asked no one in particular.

Jesse turned some of the papers back over and Ax and Sivas went back to concentrating on the metal cabinet's padlock.

"Why don't you see if you can fit through the gap," Sivas suggested to Ax.

Ax looked at the tiny slit in the metal door.

"You think I can fit through that?" he asked.

Madinal was with them now.

"Your broken wing might finally come in use," she said to Ax with a smile.

Ax knew it would be tight, but they were right, it was worth a shot. He pushed back his wings as close to his body as he could. He tried to squeeze through. It was not going to work.

"If I get through this it will be the smallest gap that I've made it through," said Ax.

"Let's see if we can help," suggested Madinal.

Sivas and Madinal got behind him and pushed. Ax kept his wing pressed flat against his side, they pushed, harder, then finally he was through.

"Phew!" he said.

Ax flew around the locker in a loop and then back up to the gap he had just squeezed through. He peered through the slit, wincing at the fresh bruise on his side, and spoke to Sivas and Madinal.

"I'll go and have a look for the syringes now," he called.

Ax flew down and went to scout the locker. He was feeling a little weak. He would just have to have a quick look and if he could not find them, he would leave, get some energy in the fairy atmosphere, then he'd come back again and have another look.

He looked underneath a stack of paper. He looked on the bottom shelf. They were not there. He went back up to the top of the locker to squeeze back through and get Sivas and Madinal to get him out. Then he saw another shelf at the top. Using a bit more energy he went all the way up. There they were. Plastic tubes with a light pink liquid inside, the thin sharp needles protected with a plastic coat. The formula was written in biro on each sticky label. Ax could not believe it.

He took a deep breath and found he was struggling to breathe. He needed to get out of the Earth's atmosphere for a moment and he needed to do it quickly.

He flew back to the small gap in the locker door, but Sivas and Madinal weren't there. They must be with Harper and Jesse. He mustered up his last bit of energy, pushed himself through the slit, which was easier this way round thanks to the slant, and fell onto the table below. He made three slow, large movements of his wing.

He lay there, but they did not come. Then he looked up at the window at the top of the room. He saw Sivas and Madinal fly out.

"Guys!" he croaked, trying his best to shout. His energy was draining. He rolled across the surface onto the next table until he was directly under the window.

"You can do it," he said to himself. "You've got this, and The Kingdom has got you."

He breathed in one more big deep breath, closed his eyes, breathed out, and pushed himself up. Up, up, right up to the window and this time he was able to grab onto the ledge. He fell through the window and rolled onto the roof to where the car had been left.

He looked up but the car wasn't there. It must be on the other side. He turned and, to his relief, saw it a little further out on the roof. Still lying on the cracked tiles, he strained and adjusted his eyes. There they were. Sivas and Madinal were in the car. What were they doing in the car? They must be waiting for him.

"I'll just be one minute," wheezed Ax, wishing one of them would come and help him into the car. He crawled towards it. Madinal and Sivas looked over at him.

"Bye, Ax," said Madinal.

"Wait, I'm getting in," said Ax.

"We're going back to Lorkun Lodge," said Sivas.

"Lorkun Lodge?" Why are you going there?" asked Ax.

"I'm a Lorkun fairy," said Madinal, looking Ax in the eye with a subtle, one-sided smile. "And now we've got the formula we wanted."

Ax felt sick.

"Sivas has moved sides and joined the Lorkun fairies," Madinal continued.

"You cannot be serious," Ax managed to say feebly.

Madinal started the engine of the car and turned to face the wheel.

"Si…" Ax trailed off, staring at the side of Sivas's head in disbelief.

Sivas glanced over at Ax, saw the pain in Ax's eyes, then quickly looked down at his seatbelt.

Madinal revved the engine and her and Sivas drove off.

Chapter Eighteen

Ax looked around him. He did not know what to do. Could he take a nap? A fairy never took a nap on Earth, but sleep would be the only thing to revive him right now. They were always told in fairy school that they couldn't take a nap in Earth's atmosphere but in this moment Ax did not believe it.

He rolled over to the sheltered side of the roof beneath an apple tree. He closed his eyes, his body was feeling weaker, and a shooting pain started pulsing through his broken wing. He tried to fall asleep, but he couldn't relax, not while his body was going into overdrive trying to bring back some of the energy he was missing.

Everything in him was trying to work faster. His muscles were in spasm, his heart was straining, and it felt as though hot spears were piercing the side of his head.

"Shouldn't my body be trying to conserve energy rather than use it?" he thought, feeling completely defeated and becoming light-headed with his energy disappearing.

It was as though his body was shutting down. He had never been this low on energy before. He imagined, for a moment, having two working wings and being able to recharge like other fairies whenever he wanted. That thought process was not helping. Why would his body not let him sleep? Or maybe it was just true that fairies could not sleep on Earth.

Ax rolled onto his back and looked up into the sky. His whole body was now in pain.

"Is this it? Is this how I die?" Ax uttered the words out loud.

No, no, no. He was not going to give in. He was not ready to die.

Ax sat up for a moment then fell back down. Another wave of nausea hit him, and he twisted onto his side, but he didn't even feel as though he would have enough energy to throw up.

Then, with every single inch of his being, pulling on every cell that was still just about awake, Ax stood and pushed up from the ground. He flew a metre in the air then fell back down with a crash.

A tear fell from his eye.

He wiped it away quickly with the back of his hand.

"I can do this."

He tried again. He got even less far this time.

"You've got this, and I've got you."

They were the words that came into his head. Words that appeared in one sentence as though from someone speaking over his left shoulder. Words that he did not realise his grandfather had said to his mother when she was pregnant with Ax and not really knowing what to do.

He pushed himself up again.

It was working. Shooting pains hit his head so hard he could not see. He pushed and pushed and pushed. He made it into the very first inch of fairy atmosphere then fell all the way back down.

But that time, those seconds in the fairy atmosphere had given him the tiniest bit of energy.

He went again.

Pain searing through every muscle, neuron, and fibre, setting them all on fire, and tugging at each atom within him, Ax pushed again.

He got a little further than last time and dropped back down.

He went again.

He got further.

He could feel his energy building up.

On the fifth time he got fully up into the fairy atmosphere, finally gaining enough energy to stay there. The pain began to dissipate in one side of his body, and the relief came through in big deep breaths.

He stayed there for a moment. Right, what was he to do now? Sivas and Madinal had gone back up to The Kingdom.

Sivas.

The look on Sivas' face flashed through his mind and, again, Ax could not believe it.

"Forget about it," he said to himself. "You are better off without them."

It did not feel true right now, but it was the only way he could deal with the betrayal.

Ax remembered where he was, and his thoughts went back to the task in hand.

He had come up with a plan.

If Madinal and Sivas were going straight to Lorkun Lodge, then he needed to get back down on Earth and help Harper and Jesse as quickly as possible. Full of strength now, he knew he needed to go and destroy the syringes and chemical formula and ought to be able to topple over the locker that contained them. They would shatter beneath him when it fell.

If all the injections were destroyed, and Madinal had taken the paper with the formula on, then there would be no need to continue the war. There would be nothing for Lorkun Lodge to fight over. The Kingdom and the humans would no longer be a threat to Lorkun Lodge. There would be peace. The humans would not be beautiful and free but maybe that was fine if it meant there was no more fighting above them in the fairy lands. They would have what they wanted without having to kill more fairies.

He flew back down to Marlborough High. This time he was going to fly back up to the fairy atmosphere regularly – just far enough to reenergise – rather than leaving it to the last minute and relying on someone to help him.

He didn't mind. It was what he always used to do.

He flew to the shabby building round the back of the school. He paused at the window which was slightly open and listened to the conversation.

"I won't be long," said Harper.

She had her coat and a backpack on and was tightening the straps of the bag.

"Have you got it on you?" asked Jesse.

"I've got everything I need," she said.

"Okay, I think the car is waiting. He's been paid all the way to Oxford."

"I have the postcode for the college if he needs it," said Harper.

"Good luck," said Jesse.

Harper nodded with a smile, standing straight, and started walking towards the door. She turned to look at Jesse.

"It's gonna be all right," she said.

"Harper," said Jesse, "Just because Uncle Henry found the address on the blueprint chemical, doesn't mean we are going to like what we find at the college. Call me if you need help."

"Okay," said Harper, then she turned and walked off.

Chapter Nineteen

The Elders walked into the out-of-bounds room. The gold was still glowing, not reflecting Maye's mood. She looked up at them.

"He managed to get some energy back," said Elson.

Maye's shoulders dropped slightly, relieved. But she did not fully relax.

"Where is he now?" she asked.

The Elders looked at each other. Maye looked at them one at a time.

"He's gone back," said Elson.

"Gone back where?" asked Maye.

"To the school," said Erin.

Elba and Elson carefully avoided eye contact with Maye.

Maye began pacing up and down the short length of the coffee table.

"And Sivas and Madinal? Did they come here?" she asked.

"They have come here just briefly. They are in Sivas's area now. They have gone into the music room," explained Elba.

"We think they're just dropping stuff off and recalibrating before going to Lorkun Lodge," added Elrin.

Maye was still moving up and down but didn't appear to react.

"Are they going straight to Vantar?" she asked.

"We assume so, yes," said Elrin.

"They have enough information," added Elson.

A message alert sounded in the room. They looked at each other but didn't say anything. They knew it would be from Vantar.

Elson walked over to pick up the message. Maye turned and flew to look out the window, her back turned to the Elders.

Elson read the message out.

It's over. We have the formula and know where it is stocked. Don't worry, it's what Axone would have wanted.

Instantly Maye spun round.

"What Axone would have wanted? What Axone would have wanted?!" her voice was rising. "They know full well it was what he fought against."

The Elders looked at Maye.

"They know full well he died trying to stop that from happening!" Maye was shouting now. "Keeping it away from Lorkun Lodge is what *killed* him." She collapsed onto a chair below the window, pressed her thumb to her forehead, and closed her eyes.

The Elders looked at each other but didn't say anything.

Maye lifted her head and opened her eyes, then began hovering above the chair a little.

"But they don't have it yet, anyway, do they?" she questioned the Elders. "I thought you said Sivas and Madinal were still here?"

"They do not have it yet," said Elson. "I think they are just playing mind games with you and know they will have it soon."

"They are feeling confident," added Elrin.

"What's Ax going to do?" asked Maye.

"He's trying to help," said Elba.

"To help Harper and Jesse," Maye sighed, instantly understanding. "Oh, why did he feel the need to get involved with those students?"

"He's got his grandfather in him," said Elson. "He can't ignore something if he thinks it is for the benefit of the humans. He has deep love for them."

"But Maye," said Elrin, "he's not doing what we thought he would. He's trying to destroy the chemical formula, not get it to all the humans."

"His grandfather tried to get it to all the humans," said Maye. "Do you know why he's doing this? Is it in the plan?"

"We have never known the details of the plan. Only what you were told by the Earthmaker in this room when Axone Junior was born."

Maye stared right through the Elders and spoke softly.

"The plan of my very own son's destiny," she said.

"Ax doesn't know any of it," said Elrin.

"And I it need to stay that way," said Maye, standing up straight with a smidgeon of resolve. "I have no right to control or change people's destiny."

"There's one more thing," said Elson. "Harper and Jesse have found the college address on one of the blueprints."

Maye's eyes widened.

"Harper has gone to look at it and Jesse has stayed back to prepare the final details for the event," said Elson.

"Oh, my goodness. What do they know?" asked Maye.

"Nothing at the moment. Only that they think there might be more of the formula hidden in the specified location within the college."

"They don't know what truly lies there?" asked Maye.

"Even if they find the box, they shouldn't be able to access the document," said Elrin.

"Please, continue to watch Ax," said Maye, expressionless. "Please continue to watch my son."

Chapter Twenty

The thought of going back to the Oxford college with Harper hit Ax with a shot of intense desire, but he decided it was too risky. He would stay with Jesse to monitor proceedings. He was still confused about what had just happened with Madinal and Sivas.

Ax didn't know why Harper was going to Oxford. The decision had been made when he was trying to get back up to the fairy atmosphere to recharge. What he did know was that, if there was a second batch of the formula somewhere, it would be best if Lorkun Lodge never, ever knew about it. It would give them further reason to fight.

However, now that Jesse was on his own, Ax was unsure about how he would destroy the syringes. He didn't want to scare Jesse with a mysterious attack. Unexplained acts from fairies made big news on Earth. If anything was healed, moved, or destroyed the humans got nervous. Careless fairies could render a house haunted forever with just a mere movement of a piece of cutlery or the closing of a door. Ax did not want an attempt to topple the locker and break the syringes to put Jesse more on edge than he already was.

There was another, bigger, reason Ax was reluctant to destroy the syringes. What if his grandfather had been right and the best thing to do was get them the humans, even if the consequences were wildly unpredictable? What if the best thing was not preventing the humans from being injected in a desperate bid for peace?

Jesse sat at the desk in the middle of the room, tapping away on his laptop, a look of deep concentration on his face. Ax flew over, landing just to the right of the screen.

He looked at Jesse rather than at the screen. He had always been fascinated by Jesse and since the project with Harper had been launched, that fascination had only increased.

Jesse was so different to Harper, yet they had both been on Ax's radar since he was a young fairy. They lived with a different sort of energy to most humans. Ax wondered what enabled them to do something no one else was willing to do. He wondered how they became so much braver than the others. He looked from Jesse to the laptop and back to Jesse who leant back, arched his spine, and stretched out his arms, then sat back up and carried on typing. What was in them that made them care so much about the potential for freedom for humans that meant they didn't feel, or could ignore, their fear? Ax wished he could ask them.

He jumped lightly onto Jesse's right forearm and climbed up to sit on his shoulder. He breathed a little fairy life onto the side of his head. Jesse brushed the hair away from his ear, having felt a slight tickle, but otherwise remained still, continuing to type. Ax flew up higher and sat on the top of Jesse's head. He sprinkled fairy peace into his hair. Little bits jumped off, landing on his shoulders and on his chest.

Being able to make humans feel these moments of contentment, peace, or joy, was one of the greatest pleasures for a fairy. They would do it more often if it were possible, but the dust would not settle on a human body while their mind was preoccupied with negativity. Only on very few occasions could fairy dust stick to pessimism. If it ever did, a sudden wave of happiness inexplicably came over the human which was exhilarating to watch.

But Ax had to be careful. Doing this used up energy.

He stayed with Jesse a moment longer and then, feeling slightly light-headed, flew over to the window. With one big push he went up to the fairy atmosphere and recharged before going back down to the school. This time around, without Madinal or Sivas to help, Ax was being incredibly careful.

He settled back on the desk and began watching the laptop screen. After a few minutes of tweaks to poster designs, emails to various convention speakers, and the simple deletion of many interview requests from journalists, a message came through on the bottom right of Jesse's screen. It was from Harper.

Jesse clicked on the notification to open it.

"There's a box here. I've opened it."

Jesse typed a response, "….?!"

"There's no formula in it."

"!"

Three dots appeared on the screen. Harper was typing.

"?" Jesse was impatient.

"But there's something else I've managed to get. It's a document."

"What is it?!?!?"

"I can't say."

"!!!"

"I'm bringing it back now."

Ax was now fluttering gently close to Jesse's face. Jesse sat, staring at the computer. He closed the laptop lid and leant back in his chair. He ran his fingers through his hair, tilted his head back, kept his hands on his head, then slowly closed his eyes.

Chapter Twenty-One

Back up in The Kingdom a party was in full swing. The Kingdom regularly threw parties. The big parties would happen approximately once a month. Usually just after the full moon on Earth.

The music was a live, fifty-seven-piece orchestra with an additional jazz ensemble in the side room. All fairies were dressed in dinner jackets or ball gowns, drinking ginger ale, brandy on ice, or red wine. Music always played in The Kingdom but only parties required actual instruments, distinguishing them from the usual joyful vibe of the fairy halls.

The Elders were there with Maye who wore a golden silk dress. The queue to speak to her was as long as it always was, and every thirty seconds or so one of the Elders would have to move a fairy on so that Maye could begin talking to the next one.

Maye enjoyed this rare chance to speak to the fairies face-to-face. In the time that they interacted with her she would hear tales about their humans, about some of the scrapes the fairy had got them out of, and about instances of joy when they laughed together. Laughing was so precious to the fairies and the humans. It was a process that awoke the soul, emptying and filling it simultaneously to the most pleasing effect. "Let it go and let it be!" was what a fairy would sing over a human who experienced laughter. Maye would also hear about moments of human crying, and how the fairy would sprinkle healing dust onto the human as the tears fell while, unbeknownst to the human, the fairy would be weeping with them.

The chatter died down and the party toast began, just before the main feast was served.

Maye excused herself from the fairy she was talking to and sat with the Elders for the meal. Today's meal was a Thai green curry with ice-cold, fizzy beer on the side.

"One of my favourite meals," Elrin said to Maye, reaching for the salt and chili flakes, once dinner was served.

"Me too," replied Maye filling her deep spoon with the curry.

Sivas and Madinal were at the party and the Elders had informed Maye about their attendance.

"Okay," she had simply said, her face completely expressionless.

"On the table behind you to the right," said Elba ten minutes into the dinner.

Again, Maye did not respond. But a short moment later she stood and topped up water glasses for those who sat closest to her. She then turned around before sitting back down, stealing a glance at Sivas and Madinal in the process. Sivas looked serious, but Madinal was happily chatting away to the male fairy on the other side of her.

Maye looked at Elrin opposite her and said quietly, barely moving her lips while looking in his eyes, "We will wait," then sat down.

Elrin nodded.

The meal ended and they once again became a crowd of singing, dancing fairies. They moved onto the sweet, deep red port in their usual post-dinner thimbles.

"To the protection and release of humans who were all born to create. I will drink this and commit to sharing my energy and love with them."

Sivas and Madinal were in the corner with a large group of teenage fairies. The fairies around them listened in awe, laughing in all the right places.

Gracefully, Maye and the Elders approached the group.

"Hello," said Maye, looking at Sivas and Madinal before turning around to nod at the rest of them with a smile.

"Hi," said Sivas, unable to look Maye in the eye.

Madinal smiled back confidently, keeping eye contact with Maye. Maye looked from Madinal slowly back to Sivas, completely unfazed by Madinal's stare.

"I understand you are Sivas," said Maye.

"Yes, yes I am."

"I believe my son has been getting to know you?" she asked.

"Yes, he's really nice, we really like him, Madinal and I do," Sivas said, fiddling with the bottom of his shirt.

Maye turned to look at Madinal.

"Ah, so you have met him too?" asked Maye.

Madinal appeared slightly less confident.

"I have," she said.

"And you are Madinal," said Maye.

"Yes."

"And you're from The Kingdom, are you?" Maye asked, looking calmly into Madinal's eyes.

"Yes. I am."

Sivas continued fidgeting next to them.

Madinal slightly narrowed her eyes, still looking at Maye.

"Well, it's nice to meet you finally," said Maye. "I just wanted to say hello. And I hope you've enjoyed the food tonight."

"It was lovely," said Sivas.

"Good," said Maye with a warm smile. "We better be off, but I will see you again soon, I'm sure."

"Great," said Madinal.

Maye started to leave but then looked back over her shoulder at Madinal after one step.

"Oh," Maye added, "Just so you know – the formula is not what Vantar tells you."

She did not wait for a response and walked off.

Chapter Twenty-Two

Six days later…

The atmosphere was tense in the hut. Uncle Henry had sent Harper an email to say that, because of the travel arrangements with his trip to Mexico, he wasn't going to make the event but that he would be there the very same evening or, if not, the next day.

In a total panic, distinct from Uncle Henry's relaxed approach, Harper and Jesse had had to think of someone to help with the running of the day, including delivering important introductions to segments of the day and make general announcements. They were pleased when the Headmaster swiftly responded to their request and agreed to do it.

It was a cold morning and the low winter sun was failing to warm up the pavements, buildings, or bodies in South London. Nevertheless, the sky was bright and blue and nearly two thousand men, women, and children were waiting outside the warehouse. They had been queueing round the block for hours already. Some of them started small talk with the stranger next to them. Some of them stayed in their own thoughts and warmed their hands keeping them firmly in their pockets, peeking up at the blue sky every so often, wishing the sun would move a little higher.

At midday, the Headmaster, dressed in a white lab coat with the collar pulled up, which he thought suited the scientific nature of the day but which his wife thought was overkill, walked out of the building doors and placed a stepladder at the head of the queue. He climbed three steps until he could see over the heads of every guest on this stretch of the street.

"First we would like to say congratulations for getting tickets and thank you for waiting in the cold for this new discovery from our very own wonderful Marlborough High students," said the Headmaster, addressing the crowd in his sweet and soothing tones, the creases around his eyes deepening as he slowly smiled.

"Let us in then. It's freezing!" someone shouted from the crowd.

"Of course," said the Headmaster. "We think it will be worth your time waiting and please proceed with caution when you enter as there are so many of you. Please have your bags and tickets ready for inspection."

The Headmaster climbed down the ladder, carried it round the corner, and repeated his announcement.

Finally, the door was opened, and guests began to enter, their bags ready for inspection.

Harper and Jesse were seated by the security monitor in the dressing room and were watching ticket holders as they began to file in.

After much debate about appropriate attire, Harper was wearing tight white jeans, a silky cream shirt, and a simple silver necklace with a small butterfly on it. Jesse had decided on dark blue jeans, a thick navy crew neck jumper, and a black t-shirt underneath. Neither of them were wearing shoes, and neither of them had styled their hair, but they still had a bit of time.

The room backstage contained three wide, purple sofas, five plastic folding chairs, jars of instant coffee, small bottles of sparkling water, a box of peppermint tea, and a range of picnic-style food including sausage rolls, cucumber sticks, and a catering sized tub of hummus.

"Have you got the document?" asked Jesse.

Harper tapped the safe next to her side of the sofa.

Jesse had been checking regularly, and Harper, patiently, had tapped the safe each time, not showing any signs of annoyance and often, if Jesse continued staring at her, she would pull on the lock to demonstrate that it was still closed.

Jesse smiled each time with a nod.

"We're going to take it into the main room with us," Jesse said quietly to Harper. "When we go in. When it properly starts," he added, moving back and forth a little in his seat.

"Yes," said Harper. "I am going to put it in my jeans pocket and give it to you only if you use the code word," she reassured him.

"And what's the code word again?" asked Jesse, casually. It was a test.

"I won't tell you out loud," she said, passing it.

They went back to watching the security monitor.

More people. Women in their fifties. Men in their twenties. Teenagers with phones out and no coats on. A wide range of body sizes, ages, skin tones, genders, and different energies. Loners. Groups.

"All these people— they're all invested in us," said Jesse. "This is so cool."

"Yeah," said Harper. "So, this is what people who want to be free from worrying about their appearances look like."

"This is what the people who have decided to trust us look like," said Jesse. "I've never felt so popular before."

"Imagine how I feel," said Harper.

Jesse looked at her and smiled. She didn't notice.

"Freedom from their looks and, after today, more freedom than they could have imagined," said Harper.

"If they buy the injection," reminded Jesse.

"Don't worry. These people are here to buy the injection," said Harper.

Chapter Twenty-Three

The first talks of the day had begun, and people had organised themselves into their preferred interest groups. The talks about hair and make-up, fashion, nature, art, and animals were spread around the large warehouse. Each topic had a speaker who was an expert in their field but knew nothing about the product Harper and Jesse had created. Each speaker explored ways in which the golden ratio was either naturally or purposefully used in their expertise to increase beauty and success, along with some ideas about how the event goers could use the golden ratio to monetise some ideas themselves.

The participants were hearing everything they wanted to hear. How to be rich, how to be successful, and how to make friends. The three things that they believed helped you become happy. Everyone with a ticket was booked in to hear the last talk of the day, delivered by Harper and Jesse and titled simply, "*How To Be Beautiful*".

They drank from thin, white plastic cups filled with instant coffee or sweet breakfast tea while they sat and listened in their groups. The mass of people soon warmed the large room. Some were making notes with a free *Divine Proportion* pen and notepad. Some were recording voice notes on their phones. Others were just listening intently.

Claps and cheers ran around the open-plan convention centre as the small-group talks wrapped up just before lunch and Harper and Jesse's favourite buffet food was served. Egg mayo, peanut butter and jam, and cheese and pickle sandwiches had been cut into triangles and laid out on the long plastic tables. Crisps, grapes, and mini sausage rolls were added to two thousand paper plates and more hot drinks were poured into a fresh round of white plastic cups.

Following lunch, guests had the chance to test out the rules of the golden ratio with the help of a professional. Some were cutting and sewing clothes. Some were applying and removing make-up. Some were drawing animals.

Harper and Jesse ventured out from the backstage area.

"Follow me," Jesse said to Harper. "I'll show you how it's done."

"Can't wait," Harper replied, reluctantly following behind.

"Be nice," said Jesse.

"I will," said Harper with a smile.

They moved from group to group, telling punters they were "over the moon" to meet them, that it was "such a pleasure," and that they were "pleased you're coming to the talk later". As they departed each group Jesse told them that it would "be nice to see a friendly face in the audience later."

Those who were already in love with Harper and Jesse could barely speak in response.

Everyone else became newly enamoured as they engaged with the pair for the first time. Harper's relaxed silence and Jesse's verbal skills, coupled in both cases with warm eye contact, were casting a spell on everyone they met.

Then, on the other side of the room, while Harper and Jesse were talking to a group at the nature table, there were two quick, loud bangs and a crash.

It sounded as though someone had hit the floor.

They both looked up, looked at each other with concern, then finished off their conversation.

"Lovely to meet you," said Jesse. "We look forward to seeing you at the talk. It will be nice to have a friendly face in the audience," he added with a wink and huge grin.

The besotted event goers fumbled a goodbye and Harper and Jesse jogged backstage to find out what had happened, picking up the pace as soon as they felt people were no longer watching.

Two security guards, on seeing Harper and Jesse approach the dressing room, rushed over to talk to them.

"There you are. We were coming to get you."

"What happened?" asked Jesse, walking briskly over to the sofa where the Headmaster and another security guard were standing.

There was a boy lying on the sofa.

"He found the syringes," said the Headmaster, looking up when he heard them.

Harper and Jesse looked at each other, horror filling their eyes.

"What's he done with them?" asked Harper.

"He's used them," said the Headmaster.

"Them? On who?" asked Jesse.

"On himself," said the Headmaster.

"More than one?!" exclaimed Jesse.

"How did he know where to put them?" asked Harper.

"He didn't," said the Headmaster.

Harper and Jesse moved closer to the boy who they could now see was unconscious. The Headmaster gently lifted the bottom half of the blanket. Harper and Jesse both gasped.

"He's put them in his leg," said Harper.

They were staring at his leg which was filled with huge, moving lumps.

"What do you want to do?" the security guard asked.

"I don't know. Is he in danger?" asked Harper, looking at the Headmaster.

"He's not going to die but there are a lot of chemicals in his system right now so his whole body is in shock," said the Headmaster. "I've done many first aid training courses and we're going to have to send him to the hospital if the swelling doesn't go down soon. But he's fine at the moment. Your Uncle

Henry is just about to call me back. We have already worked out that they haven't been injected in the right place to make him beautiful or let him see beauty."

"Okay," said Harper.

"Don't leave his side," said Jesse. "And let us know if anything changes. But we need to carry on."

"I agree," said Harper. "A lot of people have come to see us. We'll make a point of highlighting the dangers of doing it yourself. It's now even more important that we talk to these people and explain all we know about the product," she added, pushing her glasses up on her nose.

Chapter Twenty-Four

Ax was flying around Harper and Jesse and had overheard the whole conversation. He decided to stay with the sick boy for a moment, thinking that he would join Harper and Jesse on the main stage when they gave their talk in the final part of the day.

Security guards were stationed by the rest of the syringes and Harper and Jesse had ordered a check of the CCTV to find out how this boy had got hold of them.

The guard on duty said he had turned his back for mere seconds and that the boy had been behaving strangely. But with such a serious reaction a lot more information would be needed when the boy came round.

The Headmaster was on one of the plastic chairs which he had pulled close to the sofa. Ax went and sat on the Headmaster's shoulder who had the stethoscope from the well-equipped first aid kit in his ears and was listening to the boy's heartbeat.

Ax was trying to work out what was going on and what he could do. He was certain that the right thing now was to get the formula out, allow the humans to be injected and let them become beautiful, and free to see beauty in everyone and everything in their world, just as his grandfather had tried to.

But this boy had already become so obsessed with the thought of guaranteed beauty that he had used an injection without knowing what he was doing. This was the sort of behaviour that would presumably only be magnified once the injections became more well known.

He fluttered off the Headmaster's shoulder and made the journey up to the fairy atmosphere to reenergise. He thought more while he lay there, stocking up on energy.

He thought about Harper and Jesse who understood the importance of freedom. They knew all the risks, many of which affected only them, and yet they carried on with it.

Ax's grandfather had fought for exactly the same freedom and had died for the cause. Lorkun Lodge did not want the chemical formula to be accessible because knew its potential threat to their power, and were waging war over it.

Ax felt his grandfather must be correct. The humans should have access to the injection. Ax had been trying to destroy the syringes and formula in attempt to create peace. But now he wanted freedom, even if gaining it meant there must be a war.

These thoughts were still spinning around Ax's head as he flew back down from the fairy atmosphere and back into the warehouse.

The sick boy was still lying there, still in a stable condition.

Ax was just about to spill a little peaceful dust onto the boy when Sivas appeared.

Ax flew up to him then stood straight.

"Hello," said Ax.

Sivas simply looked at him and spoke as though they had never met.

"You are risking your life," said Sivas, in a matter of fact tone.

"Sivas, what happened? You betrayed me. Why did you switch sides?" Ax asked earnestly.

Sivas ignored him and continued.

"The whole of The Kingdom," said Sivas, coldly.

"What are you talking about?" asked Ax.

"We are going to destroy you. To destroy The Kingdom. To destroy the humans, to destroy the drug. To lock the humans into mortality forever. To lock them into fear."

"I am not letting go without a fight," said Ax, flying a little closer to Sivas, who backed away as he did so. "Humans and fairies can have freedom and eternal beauty. Even if the power structure gets chaotic on the way. I know the risks, Si. Harper and Jesse know the risks. But it's something worth fighting for. And you know it is, too."

"You don't get it, do you?" asked Sivas with a fierce glare.

"The Lorkun threat is real. Their intentions are serious, Ax."

Sivas's eyes had warmed for a split second as he said Ax's name.

"They will get what they want and what they want is to kill you. To destroy the chemical. To stop Harper and Jesse. They will win. They will rule," said Sivas.

"Just go away," said Ax.

He turned and went back to concentrating on the sick boy. He could still feel Sivas's presence and turned to look at him again.

"I want every human on this planet to live free from the hierarchy of beauty," said Ax.

"You care for them way too much," said Sivas.

"It will be worth it," said Ax. "Even if it means I die."

Chapter Twenty-Five

"He just said it," said Maye. "Did you hear that?"

The Elders nodded.

They were in the out-of-bounds room watching Ax on the TV screen.

"Oh my goodness," said Maye.

Elrin tugged at the bottom of his t-shirt. Elba shuffled his feet. Elson ran his hand through his hair.

Maye was still staring at the screen.

"I always knew I might see him die," she said. "But I never thought I would witness the moment he offered himself up."

"Those words will be taken as permission," Elson said as quietly as he could.

"It makes sense now," said Elba.

Like Maye, the Elders had not been prepared for this. In the short moments after Ax was born they had been filled, through their collective spirit, with an utter knowing that the baby Maye had just given birth to would be a sacrifice for the freedom of humans on Earth. His broken wing would help fairies understand it. It made him weaker, he inherited it from his grandfather, it removed his immortality. But there were rules of permission over life and death in The Kingdom and the Elders knew at some point Ax would have to give permission for fate to take control of his life. At the time Maye had been given the choice about whether she would allow her son to be swapped for the humans' freedom and immortality. She had always known she could withhold her permission. Despite knowing this since the day her baby was born, and despite being confident she had made the right choice, she had not been prepared for the moment in which he offered himself up with the words she had just heard him say out loud.

'Even if it means I die.'

They were still ringing in Maye's ears.

She sat down in the chair, unable, for a moment, to continue watching the screen.

She closed her eyes and thought of her father. He knew the humans were worth dying for. All fairies believed it, but most were never truly tested on their belief. Most fairies never had to make the choice. Maye opened her eyes and stood back up. Her father had to make the choice. Her son had to make the choice.

In silence she walked back up to the screen, the Elders were unmoving in silence behind her. She took a breath, breathing slowly in, then gave it away, breathing slowly out. She continued watching her son.

Chapter Twenty-Six

Ax knew he needed to get ready for battle in case what Sivas had just told him was true. He still had a lot of energy left but, nevertheless, he went back up to the fairy atmosphere once again to completely top up. There was a chance he would need it all and he was taking no risks today.

While recharging, Ax thought through what he would need to do. First, the vials that held the chemical needed checking. They needed to be secure. Second, he would need to check on Harper and Jesse. There was still one document they had which he had not been able to read, but that didn't matter right now. He would need to make sure there was no threat to Harper and Jesse's physical safety. Along with Uncle Henry, who had not even turned up and didn't seem to see a problem with missing the main event, they were the only ones who knew how to administer the injections.

Once the demonstrations were done the first humans would quickly be free.

From there, the rest should take care of itself. There was another side, however, to consider, too. Ax didn't know the specific plans of the Lorkun fairies.

Sivas's words were ringing in his head. *They will get you first.*

Ax shook off the thought. All he would have to do would be to keep the Lorkun fairies away long enough for Harper and Jesse to inject a couple of the humans. Once the first few injections were administered, the humans would have the freedom to continue alone, replicating what they had seen. The only possible problem Ax considered was that a Lorkun fairy could get between the needle and the human skin each time the chemical was about to be injected.

If it was only Sivas and Madinal, Ax would have no problem with keeping them away. If it were more than that – Ax barely allowed himself to think about it, but the image still managed to flash through his head – if it were *many* Lorkun fairies attacking, Ax would be helpless.

He considered asking his mum for help. But she had been through so much. This was his chance to help her and help The Kingdom, as well as the humans on Earth.

He did not have any fairy friends in The Kingdom to tell and after Madinal and Sivas's betrayal he was more cautious than ever. But there was one fairy he could trust.

Ax went back to the dressing room and checked on the syringes which, following the incident with the teenage boy, were now guarded by two security staff.

He then flew to check on Harper and Jesse. They were talking so smoothly, so calmly, belying their worries, to all the punters who had paid two hundred and fifty pounds to be at their event. They were fine, too.

Then Ax went back up to The Kingdom. He didn't want to go in, so he asked the lady on the door to tell his mum's friend Salli he needed to speak to her.

"Of course, Axone Junior. I'll fetch her right away."

A few moments later Salli flew over to him, greeting him with the warmest smile, as always, and a tight hug. Her hugs had a way of squeezing worry out of you and taking it right away.

Salli worked in the dining hall. It had been Salli who had kept the other fairies away when Ax was born. It had been Salli who had rushed him and Maye into the out-of-bounds room without others seeing them.

"You are growing up so well, Ax, look at you. Are you happy?" Salli asked, wiping a strand of Ax's hair out of his eyes.

"I am," said Ax with a smile. "But I need your help. I promise I wouldn't be asking if this wasn't really important. I think I might be in trouble."

"Goodness, of course. What is it?" she asked.

"This cannot go to my mum," said Ax before he began.

"Your secret's safe," she said, eyes wide.

Ax began to explain that he needed help. That the humans on Earth were soon going to be beautiful and free from longing for what they thought they did not have. That he believed the Lorkun fairies may be planning to try and stop the injections. That he did not know how many Lorkun fairies there would be. That Harper and Jesse were two humans he had been watching for years. That Sivas and Madinal had betrayed him and The Kingdom, were on the side of Lorkun Lodge, and knew more than he would like. That this was finally a chance to finish what Axone had been determined to do. That this was the war Axone had started and that this time it could be won and finally, that before he could win, he needed her help.

Chapter Twenty-Seven

Ax was back down on Earth in the dressing room with Harper and Jesse. He felt nervous about his plan but since seeing Salli in The Kingdom adrenaline had been flowing throughout his fairy body and, if timings went well, there was no reason he could think of why his plan would not work.

Ax began thinking about seeing his mum when this was all over. He was starting to miss her. But he was doing this for her. And for his grandfather. She would not understand if he tried to explain his plan now but, when it was over, he would easily be able to explain it to her. Soon it would all make sense.

Harper was sitting on one of the white plastic chairs, dipping a custard cream into her tea. Jesse was drinking a black coffee and styling his hair while they read through the final draft of their speech.

Once they were happy with it, Harper checked her jeans pocket for the document she had taken from the college. Yep, it was still there. Jesse saw her check it and gave her a little smile and a nod. His toe was tapping beneath the dressing table. They had moved the document from the safe to Harper's jeans' pocket only five minutes ago.

Harper opened Jesse's laptop to see how the press coverage had been ramping up.

One channel was live streaming the event from outside the convention building.

"There's a live stream from the outside," said Harper.

"That must be a boring show," said Jesse, shaking his head while pulling his right foot up onto his left knee, then holding his ankle with both hands.

"No way is anyone watching that," said Harper, pushing her glasses up on her nose.

She clicked on the link. Harper immediately sat up straighter.

"There are over one hundred thousand people viewing it," said Harper, looking up at Jesse.

"No way," said Jesse.

She began to read the comments to Jesse.

'15mins to go.'

'I can't wait 2 see them.'

'Can someone pls tell me what they are wearing?'

'I love u!'

'Can I be your guinea pig?'

'What happened to the boy who passed out lol?'

Harper and Jesse froze on the words 'passed out'.

"How can they know?" asked Jesse.

"I don't know," said Harper. "Hang on."

She tapped four words into the search bar and started scrolling through the news articles that appeared.

One site had reported a boy passing out, however, the author was just a random blogger and so it seemed as though most people had chosen to ignore it, and assumed the boy had just become dehydrated or over excited and fainted.

The comment on the live stream must have just been from one person who wasn't fussy about their sources.

Still, reading the comment had made Harper and Jesse more nervous.

What if a journalist asked them about it during the press conference afterwards?

Harper and Jesse whispered to each other, their faces clearly telling everyone in the dressing room to give them space and not listen in.

They decided they'd admit that it was true, he fainted, and that they were very flattered people found them so interesting and got so excited, but they were very boring students really and they wished him well. Jesse would then blow a kiss to the camera and wink while Harper smiled and laughed a little, just enough to encourage the journalists to laugh with them and convince them they had just witnessed Jesse do something funny, or to simply lighten the mood.

Harper and Jesse went to the sofa and checked on the boy again. They were relieved to hear the Headmaster say the boy had regained consciousness but was sleeping off the shock and some of the effects of the chemical formula still in his system.

Chapter Twenty-Eight

Madinal and Sivas were in Lorkun Lodge. The walls were dark and, although music played naturally through the walls, just as it did in The Kingdom, the fairies in Lorkun Lodge did not naturally all sing along with it.

Lorkun Lodge was much bigger than The Kingdom and the fairies had their own bedrooms in which they spent a lot of their time. They had communal dinners, but they were not unanimously attended the way they were in The Kingdom.

"Why would we all go to dinner every day when we can get unlimited pizzas created right in our bedrooms?" said Madinal, posing the rhetorical question to Sivas when he first arrived at Lorkun Lodge.

They were now seated on Madinal's bed with an exact replica of an Earthly hot 'n' spicy delivery-style pizza between them, the thick crust gently squishing in their hands as they pulled each piece, a little oil dripping onto the box, and the scent of pepperoni hitting their noses with each bite.

"Vantar knows he owes you big time," said Madinal, wiping her left-hand fingers on a piece of paper towel before reaching for another slice. "Helping us out like this."

"Oh, I don't mind about that," said Sivas, baffled by the comment.

"Well, he knows it and don't worry. Fairies get rewarded here. Not like in The Kingdom where they claim they do not want rewards."

"I did it just because it was the right thing to do," said Sivas. "I'm proud to be a member of Lorkun Lodge. You are fighting for what's right."

Madinal stared at Sivas. She smiled.

"Good," she said.

Sivas reached for another slice of pizza.

"You're going to be a good Lorkun fairy," said Madinal. "I wouldn't be surprised, and this doesn't go further than between you and me, if Vantar was planning on making you a top fairy after this. After the war is over."

"Is he making you a top fairy?" asked Sivas.

"Yes. But nobody knows about this. So don't say anything yet," said Madinal.

"Wow. Vantar really is rewarding you," said Sivas. "And me?" he asked. "Do you think what I've done could get me promoted to top fairy, too?"

"We couldn't have done any of this without you. We are now able to attack The Kingdom fairies *and* stop the humans becoming free and immortal all thanks to you," said Madinal. "We owe you a lot. You will no doubt be put in charge in some form forever."

Sivas looked down at his slice of pizza. He moved a piece of pepperoni so it wasn't hanging off the edge, and lifted the slice to his mouth.

"I am sure Vantar will have many more big plans for you," Madinal continued. "Even when we win this war, there will be more battles to come with other fairy lands in the future. The Kingdom fairies will not go down without a fight. We know that. But you have shown you are loyal, and we know we can trust you."

She picked up her cold bottle of beer – one of her favourite Earth drinks to replicate – from the bedside table but hesitated before putting the green glass to her lips.

"You've made the right choice," she said, then lifted the bottle and took a big gulp.

She looked at Sivas. "Cheers," she said, thrusting her bottle towards him.

Sivas reached for his cold lager, clinked it against hers, then they sipped their drinks.

"Enjoy this pizza," said Madinal, beginning to stand up and placing her beer back down. "The war is about to begin."

Just then, a message came beeping through on the grey machine on the desk in Madinal's room.

She flew over to look at it and read out the message.

Meet in the great hall in half an hour.

She sat back down on the bed with Sivas.

"A lot of our fairies do not know what it's for," she said. "But they do whatever Vantar says and trust that he always knows best. It's how all fairies have been trained here since they were babies."

Madinal and Sivas made their way towards the great hall.

It was already filled with thousands of Lorkun fairies chatting and waiting to hear what all the fuss was about. Rumours had been circulating all afternoon.

Vantar flew in above their heads just as Sivas and Madinal were approaching the door and the three of them flew in towards the crowd together.

Their entrance created a hush.

They flew to the stage and hovered above it, facing the crowd. Sweat began trickling down Sivas's neck while Madinal remained confidently poised on the other side of Vantar as he began to address the fairies.

"There is a convention," he said, his voice ringing across the great hall, "happening down on Earth organised by two school students. They are administering injections to every human who wants their face to fall in line with the golden ratio, also known as divine proportion. It makes everything, and soon every*one*, beautiful. Regardless of personal taste, cultural experiences, or social constructions the ratio is attractive."

The fairies listened in awe. It was rare that they got to see Vantar, their leader, in the flesh or to hear his voice.

"But this injection is not good for them. Once they can see beauty in everything there will be a confused and angry mentality. They will no longer respect their elders or those who have been duly elected to oversee their safety. They will no longer value rare beauty, or money, or possessions, or any other structures created to keep them under control. There will, with the illusion of inequality taken away, be no reason for them to work hard and to earn more money than they need in an attempt to become equal. My fairies, I am sure you do not need me to tell you what a disaster this will be. For us and for them. They will become angry and they will fight. We have already seen the trials in mice. The Kingdom does not understand this. They think universal beauty for the humans is worth it, even if they will have no structure, no control, and may become angry. That is why I am calling all of you to come with me to the event and get in the way of every injection administered. We will not allow one single human to be injected with this *poison*."

As Vantar spat the last word the crowd cheered.

"There are thousands of us and, as far as we know, there will only be one fairy from The

Kingdom. Ax is alone and he will be defeated easily, just as his grandfather was."

They cheered again.

Sivas wondered why Vantar had not mentioned that the injection also meant humans would become immortal after dying, moving up into The Kingdom's vibrational state, gaining access to the new world. He knew Vantar would have a good reason for it.

The Lorkun fairies prepared to travel to Earth.

Chapter Twenty-Nine

Ax was in the dressing room with Salli who had brought her daughter with her.

"Hi, I'm Tiffette," she said doing a little spin, not knowing what to do with the spare energy flowing through her.

"Hi," said Ax. "Thank you for coming down."

Tiffette was younger than Ax and full of energy.

Ax was pleased to have her on their team. Even if Madinal and Sivas brought as many as ten other fairies with them, Ax was confident that the three of them could keep the Lorkun fairies away. There was only going to be one injection at a time.

Salli was tying up Ax's bad wing with bamboo wire to help strengthen it. Strapping it back was not ideal, but he needed what help he could get, and the structure would at least help to keep it stable.

While he hovered in the air having his wing sorted out, Tiffette was whizzing around in circles above his head having already buzzed up and down, round and round, all over Harper and Jesse without them knowing when she first arrived.

"Their energy!" she exclaimed. "Their bravery! Their fearlessness!"

"I told you they were great," said Ax. "That's why I've been following them around for so long. I could have chosen any humans on Earth."

"I get it," said Salli.

"And did you know," continued Ax, "They never even used to know each other. I used to watch them separately."

Tiffette whizzed up to them again, almost slipping and falling into Harper's tea as she dunked another corner of custard cream into the steamy drink.

"I've never met anyone like them. They're choosing to be bold even when they are nervous," she said before whizzing off again.

"I couldn't believe it when they met in the corridor then started hanging out together," Ax said to Salli. "They were so different, but it made perfect sense. But now I wonder whether it *was* a good thing," he added. "It has become the most stressful time of my life," he said with a chuckle.

"But it's giving you a sense of purpose, Ax," said Salli. "And it makes so much sense, knowing your grandfather, why you do the most you can to help. Plus, you are in a position of power. People will help you, Ax. You have scared the Lorkun fairies. Vantar is not scared of others. It had to be you, sweet one."

Ax relaxed back into the final adjustments Salli was making on his wings.

"Right. You're good to go," said Salli, giving him a pat on the shoulder.

He rolled his shoulders back, testing how the new support felt.

"Thank you," he said.

"No worries. I'll be back in a minute."

Ax went over to the mirror and looked at the supported wing then went off to find Tiffette and show her more of the cool things in the dressing room.

Salli flew out of the convention building when Ax was not looking and headed back to The Kingdom.

She headed straight to the dining hall when she arrived.

"Where have you been, you look awful," Molliah said when Salli whizzed in.

"Ax is getting ready for the battle," said Salli. "He doesn't know it, but he is wholly unprepared. If we fight like this, we will lose and I think there are many coming from the Lorkun Lodge."

"Goodness. Don't worry," Molliah replied. "We will get something sorted. Go back down and we will see you very soon. Leave this with me."

Chapter Thirty

Maye was watching the screen, looking at Ax and Tiffette fluttering around the dressing room with Harper and Jesse, and she was beginning to panic.

"He isn't ready. He doesn't understand the weight of this," she said. "And he is on his own."

"He has Salli and Tiffette with him," said Elrin.

"It might not be as bad as we think," added Elba. "There might not be that many from Lorkun Lodge coming."

"The attack is going to be catastrophic," said Maye, pacing the room. "We haven't seen anything on this scale in many years. They lost the formula once, on that night in the college when they killed my father. They won't be half-hearted about it again. This time they will come to win."

"We will see what we can do," said Elson.

"You know, there is always the option," said Elrin, tentatively, "to change course. To interfere."

Maye's face dropped. "To change the course of destiny," she said quietly, "is not an option."

She moved back to look at the TV screen, watching her son on Earth in the calm of the dressing room.

"When you were told of his destiny, you were always given the option of keeping your son and not allowing the humans to be free," said Elson. "You still have that option now. It's not too late. We could warn Ax. We could take him out. Someone else could die in his place."

Maye stayed quite for a moment. She was thinking about it.

"I cannot do something so selfish," she said. "I must let him make his own choices and you heard him. He made his choice. He, like his grandfather, is willing to die for the humans so that they might become immortal. They are not just saying it. They mean it. Ax and Axone. My father and my son. You can see it in my baby's eyes, and I saw it in my dad's eyes before he died."

Maye knew she could save her son, but only if she did not believe in the importance of this destiny. Her mind was buzzing as it had been for years. If she changed her son's destiny, she would have to live knowing it was her fault the humans were not free. Because it was part of her destiny, too. It was her sacrifice, too. She had thought so much about it. She had seen her father die. She was then told she would see her son die, just after being gifted the miracle of birth. Her purpose in The Kingdom was to accept the ultimate pain and suffering, the burden of loss. To be okay with it, and to find something bigger than herself when she let go. That was what she needed to do. The humans' freedom involved letting go of what they thought they wanted on Earth. They could hardly let go and enter The

Kingdom's vibrational state, of which she was godmother, if she was not prepared to let go of what mattered to her the most first. She could not hold on any longer. Not if she wanted humans to be free. There was always a chance he would not die. But she had to be willing to let him.

Maye turned away from the screen and faced the Elders. She rolled her shoulders back and stood up straight. She closed her eyes and took a breath in. She opened her eyes and let the breath out.

"We are going to allow it to happen," she said. "You may, if you want, stand by me and watch. Nothing will change this now."

Chapter Thirty-One

Ax was in the dressing room with Tiffette and Salli who had arrived back from her trip to The Kingdom. She had not been gone long and neither Ax nor Tiffette noticed she'd been gone. Salli carried on as normal.

"You need to conserve your energy," she told Ax while Tiffette was whizzing around.

Harper and Jesse were getting ready to go on stage and deliver their speech. Jesse was retouching his hair in front of the mirror. Harper was reading over her notes and monitoring her phone. She was also checking the document in her pocket every ten seconds, or so it seemed.

A security guard walked over.

"Two minutes until you're on," he told them.

"Thank you," said Jesse.

They stood up, walked towards each other and, for the first time since selling out the tickets online, Harper and Jesse wrapped their arms around each other and relaxed.

They pulled apart, looked at each other with a straight face, then walked out towards the stage.

Before they appeared on stage there was an announcement.

"Ladies and gentlemen," said the Headmaster, putting on his authoritative teacher voice, "there will be absolutely no videos, images, or texts from now until the end of the event. We thank you for your cooperation. Any breaches of these conditions will be taken seriously, and you will be instantly removed."

Harper and Jesse peered at the crowd around the curtain behind which they stood at the side of the stage. A mum with curly hair and two little boys wearing matching tracksuits were on the front row. The boys were colouring in black and white pictures of golden ratio examples which had been given to them during the practical tasks earlier.

There were three girls two rows behind them with pocket mirrors up in front of their faces, practicing putting make-up on in accordance with the golden ratio to structure their features in a universally, objectively beautiful form.

"We won't even have to put make-up on or ever wear it again after this," said one to the other.

"After the injection?"

"Yeah."

"Well, we don't even know how much it's gonna cost yet."

"I don't think it matters. We're going to get it. It will obviously be worth every penny. There's no point coming if you don't want to get it."

A man in his fifties sat with his wife at the back of the room. They were willing to pay whatever it took to get the injection. The man was a photographer and had encountered the golden ratio before, but this was a whole new level. Then the photographer noticed three teen boys about ten rows in front them.

"I wonder why they think they need it," he said to his wife, pointing to the teenage boys. "They've got the beauty of youth."

"They might be planning to buy and sell it. These young people are very entrepreneurial you know," she said, tapping his arm gently.

The last sentence was reduced, half-way, to a whisper as everyone fell silent.

"Please welcome to the stage, I know many of you have met them today, the orchestrators of your new life changing product, something everybody deserves: beauty and the freedom that comes with it. Please welcome Marlborough High's very own Harper and Jesse."

The entire crowd rose to their feet, cheering and clapping loudly.

The excited noise tripled in volume as Harper and Jesse stepped onto the stage and, after a few minutes, the two of them became a bit awkward. Finally, Jesse got the crowd to sit down and, through a chuckle as the noise finally ended, he began to speak.

"Thank you all so much for coming," he said.

Ax was on stage with them. There was a security guard at the back of the stage with the syringes in a box.

Ax was flying confidently between Harper, Jesse, and the security guard.

Salli and Tiffette had both remained in the dressing room and were going to join Ax just before the demonstration began.

There was still no sign of Sivas, Madinal, or any of the fairies from Lorkun Lodge.

Perhaps Ax had been wrong to be concerned. This was going to be fine.

Chapter Thirty-Two

Back at Lorkun Lodge the fairies were lined up ready to go. There had been many thousands of them at the beginning of Vantar's announcement, but the numbers had gradually diminished during his speech but there were still a good few thousand.

In the final moments before they left, the Lorkun fairies were given a briefing to ensure that not one needle point would touch any human skin. They were told that this should be an easy task but that any inattention could be a disaster.

Lorkun Lodge fairies were brought up and trained never to make mistakes and to strive for perfection. Of course, it was never fully expected that you would always achieve perfection, but some got close and the important thing was that perfection was what you aimed for.

Vantar was staying back at Lorkun Lodge while the others went to fight. It was not worth the risk of him dying, he explained. Sivas and Madinal went to his office for one last word with him.

"Come in," Vantar called through the slightly ajar iron door.

They flew into his office.

"Is this all we need to do?" asked Madinal.

"It is everything you need to do. Finally, we will win, and we will conquer," said Vantar.

"Thank you for the opportunity" said Sivas.

"It's thanks to you that we are able to do this," said Vantar. "Believe me, Sivas, we know what you're doing for us and you will be greatly rewarded for it. I know Madinal may have told you what position I am promoting her to and may have hinted that your future could be the same. It is true. When this war is over, we will have a lot to discuss and you can have whatever you want. You have proven your loyalty and we will

271

celebrate with you here at Lorkun Lodge when this battle is done."

Chapter Thirty-Three

Salli was still backstage with Tiffette. They were watching Harper, Jesse, and Ax on the screen. Salli was struggling to hide her nervousness. Her eyes were darting left and right constantly across the screen while simultaneously checking for the appearance of any fairies from The Kingdom.

"Why do you keep checking behind you, Mum?" Tiffette asked. "We've got this. Don't worry."

"Sweetie, I want you to go and help Ax," Salli said to Tiffette, putting one hand lightly on her daughter's arm.

"But he hasn't given the signal," said Tiffette, "and the Lorkun fairies aren't here. They may not even turn up at all. Don't you think they would be here by now if they were going to do something?"

"They're probably on their way," said Salli, trying to wipe a bead of sweat from her forehead without Tiffette noticing, "and I think it is better that you are there, ready to help him fight off Sivas and Madinal. I'll join you at the very first sighting of any other fairies from Lorkun Lodge."

"Alright, Mum," said Tiffette. "I'll see you in a bit."

Tiffette flew out into the main hall and Salli continued watching the screen, refocused, while nervously tapping away on her knee.

"Where are they?" Salli wondered.

Just as she was beginning to lose hope, a fairy from The Kingdom flew into the backstage dressing room. Salli let out a sigh with a big grin.

Molliah grinned back and flew right up to her.

"There you are," said Salli, giving Molliah a hug.

Out of the corner of her eye Salli saw another fairy from The Kingdom enter the room.

***

Maye had begun pacing back and forth.

She had been unable to watch for the last five minutes. It was too difficult to watch Ax as he fluttered around onstage, now also with Tiffette, completely unaware of the number of fairies that were about to attack.

"Tiffette will be dead, too," Maye whispered.

She was still pacing around the room while the Elders watched the screen.

"Tell me if anything happens," Maye instructed. "Tell me when they start to fight. I don't know if I will be able to watch but I want to know what is happening."

"Maye," said Elson, flying up to her, "fairies are arriving."

"Lorkun fairies?" asked Maye.

"No," said Elson. "Fairies from The Kingdom. Our fairies. They are turning up backstage now. Ax doesn't know yet. There are thousands of them."

Excitedly, but nervous in case it wasn't true, Maye flew up to the screen to see for herself. Elba stood to the side so that she could look at the screen.

"There are so many of them," she said. "Who did this?"

"Salli. She knew that Ax needed backup. She is looking out for him," said Elba.

The fairies from The Kingdom were flying into the backstage area in a hushed excitement, many of them hugging Salli as they arrived, all of them happy and filled with energy to start fighting the battle for Ax.

Maye and the Elders were staring at the screen. Maye was now watching with a smile on her face, each breath in making her feel as though she was going to burst through overwhelming love for The Kingdom fairies.

"Where are they all coming from?" Maye asked. "I haven't seen anything like this before. They are all getting ready to go out and do battle with Ax."

She continued to look as more and more fairies poured in. Her baby had back up. Her baby still didn't know the extent of the threat, but her baby would have help to fight in this war.

She was now tapping on the side of the screen, unable to break away as more fairies from The Kingdom continued to fly in.

"Goodness me," Maye whispered. "Our fairies are rising up."

Chapter Thirty-Four

Maye asked Elson to zoom in on The Kingdom fairies in the dressing room backstage.

He clicked a couple of buttons and the scene backstage appeared in magnified detail.

Mothers were there dressing their children in support cloth, ready for battle. Fathers were showing their daughters how to fire the straightest arrow, giving them advice on moves they had learnt while fighting in the wars. Those who had been in the battle at the college were telling stories about Axone's bravery and his dedication to the humans and the cause. Many of the younger fairies who had showed up had been in school with Ax. They were talking about how he had loved all humans ever since they could remember and weren't surprised that he was leading this. All of them had been informed by Salli on what the injection was capable of and some of them were now discussing the details amongst themselves. How it worked. How cool it was.

Salli then explained that the Lorkun fairies were coming in great numbers to prevent the injection being administered and to destroy the formula afterwards, and that they were determined and smart, but that they believed Ax was on his own.

Chapter Thirty-Five

Harper and Jesse had been talking for nearly an hour. The crowd, after cheering through the first ten minutes of the speech, had settled down and absorbed everything they said.

The crowd laughed and gasped when Harper and Jesse told anecdotes about eating and washing in the shabby hut in the school grounds; and about going home to sleep for a mere two hours before meeting back at the hut, pouring Italian coffee from the lonesome kettle in the corner, then carrying on working on the product. The crowd were totally silent and unmoving when Harper and Jesse spoke about their conversation with the Headmaster who decided whether or not they could carry on promoting the product from the school and how close the project had come to being cancelled.

The crowd absorbed the surface layer of Harper and Jesse with all the correct reactions. But no one there could tell how

Harper and Jesse were feeling underneath. No one noticed Harper tapping her jeans pocket every thirty seconds or Jesse darting his eyes to Harper's hand each time she did it. They simply noticed how calm, relaxed, funny, and charming Harper and Jesse were.

Despite his mind racing, Ax had managed to conserve much of his energy by standing still in the corner of the stage as he watched the students talk to the crowd. Tiffette, however, was darting around the audience, fascinated by all the humans who were here to watch the demonstration.

"Thank you for listening to us today," Jesse addressed the crowd. "And now, finally, for the part you have been waiting for. The only reason you came. We are going to perform a demonstration of the product."

The cheering and whooping began all over again, along with a few excited gasps, and much rustling and shuffling in seats, all with a new urgency than had been felt at the beginning of the talk.

"We are going to need three volunteers," Harper said when the room quietened a little. "Which means three of you will get the injection for free," she continued. "We have generated a list of your names from the ticketing system and there is now going to be a random selection process which holds no bias for any of your features or personality traits."

"If you don't wish to take part in the demonstration," Jesse chipped in, "that's no problem, we will simply move on and pick another person."

Jesse tapped 'Start' on the screen which visually mimicked a lottery turn ball on the projection behind them. There was total silence while it spun. Then a name appeared.

SANDRA KAYWOOD

"No way!" said Sandra, standing up in her seat.

Her friends began squealing, pulling at her arms, and touching her waist.

"Go, go," said one friend.

"You've got to go," said another.

Sandra pushed her bag under her seat, handed her jacket to her friend, and began to walk between the chairs out into the aisle. Her friends who remained seated began hugging.

"Sandra would you like to take part in the demonstration?" Jesse asked into the microphone.

"Yes!" said Sandra, already walking down the aisle.

"Come on up to the platform!" said Harper.

"Let's spin again while Sandra makes her way up here," said Jesse.

Ax was watching Sandra walk down the aisle between the rows of chairs toward the stage. Then, out of the corner of his eye, coming towards him, Ax saw Sivas.

Sivas was on his own and was heading straight for the centre stage where the demonstration was taking place. Ax stole a couple of quick glances at him but did not want to take his eyes off Sandra for too long.

Sivas caught Ax's eye but then went flying straight past him to the other side of the stage.

Ax turned around and flew after Sivas.

"Only a few more minutes until the demonstrations begin," Harper announced.

Ax caught up with Sivas who stopped flying when Ax reached him.

"I thought you would at least bring Madinal with you," said Ax. "Where is she?"

"She's coming," said Sivas. "And so are others."

"Okay, well done. Because you might need help with this one," said Ax, not smiling at all. "You know it's not too late for you to change your mind."

Sivas looked Ax in the eye properly for the first time since they had last been together. There was a momentary warmth back in Sivas's eyes.

"I can't. It's not what's best for the people," said Sivas.

Ax sighed and looked away.

"If you believe that, if you truly believe that, then let the battle begin," said Ax.

"I want you to be safe, Ax. I think you should go away," said Sivas.

"No way. No way am I doing that," said Ax. "You just want an easy win. My grandfather fought for this and I am going to fight for this. I am not going to let you have your way. I am not going to run or stand back. I am going to finish what my grandfather began before he was killed in the attempt."

"Okay." Sivas looked at Ax with a nod. "I tried to warn you. But have it your way."

Ax looked at Sivas. "I'm not afraid," he said.

Sivas shook his head. "You will die for the humans because you care too much, and we will win."

Then Sivas flew off.

Ax was filled with excitement now. When he had told Sivas that he was not afraid, it had become true. He breathed calmly. He zoomed out in his thoughts and focused on the big picture and what he was fighting for. He thought of his grandfather. He thought of the humans. He thought of The Kingdom. And then he saw Sivas fly back into the room.

A few seconds later Madinal came in behind him.

Behind her another Lorkun fairy followed.

And another.

And a few more.

Ax began to panic.

"Tiffette!" he called. "We need your mum."

Chapter Thirty-Six

Tiffette had in fact already called Salli and by the time Ax had finished his sentence she was there with them. The Lorkun fairies were nearly at them and as Salli approached Ax, she spoke.

"Don't worry, we've got this," she said.

Ax turned around to look back at the Lorkun fairies, and then heard a gentle humming sound coming from behind Salli.

He looked back and there they were. Fairies from The Kingdom coming in one great big long line, glowing with utter radiance and ultra-energy.

Ax looked back at Harper and Jesse.

"We have all three of the volunteers for the demonstration now and we are ready to begin!" said Jesse.

Harper walked over to the security guard with the box of syringes and brought the whole box forward.

"Sandra, you were first. We'll start with you," said Jesse.

Sandra and the other two participants were sitting on stools in the centre of the stage. They had confirmed their names in front of the crowd and had confirmed that they wanted to go ahead with the procedure.

"You are about to see how easy and pain-free this is, and you will also, of course, see the results," said Jesse.

He smiled at Sandra and asked, quietly, "Are you okay? Are you ready to begin?"

Sandra nodded at Jesse with a smile.

Sivas now had Madinal at his side, and they were hovering in front of Ax. Ax had Salli and Tiffette by *his* side and The Kingdom fairies were gathering behind them.

"You only have moments," said Ax, "before these humans are injected and the course of the world is changed, just as it ought to be, forever."

Madinal shook her head with a subtle smirk on her face.

"We have many fairies with us, Ax. If you think we'll let you inject these humans today, you are wholly mistaken," she said.

Madinal turned to the Lorkun fairies that were gathering behind her and Sivas, her back now to Ax.

"The injections are about to begin. Do not let the needle pierce the skin," she instructed them.

She whipped her head round to look at Ax.

"Don't think we are going to let one injection get to a human," she said.

Ax turned around to see The Kingdom fairies. He couldn't believe it. They were still arriving.

"Our fairies will ensure the injections go in," he said to Madinal, straight-faced.

Ax and Madinal both looked over at Harper.

"Okay, Sandra," said Harper, "the first injection will be just above the brow."

Harper was drawing navy blue dots on Sandra's head where the needle was going to go.

Lorkun fairies began to fly toward Sandra and Harper.

Ax turned around to the thousands of fairies behind him. He looked at Sivas who was showing no signs of fear then back to The Kingdom fairies.

"My fairies of The Kingdom," Ax said to them. "Attack."

They began zooming right past Ax up to the Lorkun fairies. The Kingdom fairies batted the first few Lorkun fairies away and the Lorkun wings were easily broken. Ten Lorkun fairies instantly dropped to the ground, unable to fly back up. Without their wings for recharging their energy, and having been hit by another immortal being, they would soon die.

The rest of the Lorkun fairies were flying around the stage. Dozens of them stood on Sandra's head, ready to jump down on her face in the way of the injection. Ax flew over with Salli and Tiffette to help get the Lorkun fairies out of the way. As they got there, he fired three arrows into a line of three Lorkun fairies who fell in screeching pain, before landing and tumbling through the crack in the stage where the platforms joined.

The needle almost went in on Harper's first attempt, but three Lorkun fairies stopped it.

Harper was confused as to why she could not get the point of the needle to pierce the skin but put it down to nerves. She stretched her hand, took a deep breath, and got ready to try again.

Salli was shoving the younger Lorkun fairies out the way. The battle going on between them had already caused casualties on both sides, but The Kingdom were winning.

Sivas was going up to control the injection area now. Many Lorkun fairies had already either been killed or were busy fighting fairies from The Kingdom elsewhere on the stage.

Ax saw his opportunity and flew over to where Sivas was.

"Sivas, move out of the way," said Ax.

"No."

"Move out of the way," Ax repeated. "It doesn't have to be like this."

"No, Ax."

"Sivas move out of the way. You are stopping something you know is good for the humans. Why are you doing this? You're scared of the chaos that might happen at first, before they go on to live with their freedom?"

"Ax, I am not moving. It is you who needs to get out of the way."

"It will be difficult and messy but then they will have options. They will have freedom. They will find the place in themselves that is content. It won't be as bad as you say it is."

"Ax, you don't know about the trial that killed one of the humans, do you?"

"There wasn't one like that."

"You haven't seen the document in Harper's pocket, have you?"

"I am sure Harper and Jesse know what they're doing. They will have made the right decision. They are doing this for the humans."

"Ax, move out of the way. MOVE OUT OF THE WAY!" Sivas screamed.

And with that an arrow came straight at Ax from behind, through his wing, through his right shoulder, and into his heart.

In the initial shock, Ax did not notice the arrow Madinal had fired at him.

"Ax!" Sivas shouted.

In that moment, the first injection went into Sandra's skin, the whole audience cheered, and Ax fell to the floor.

Sivas swooped down to catch him.

Madinal flew down to follow him.

"What are you doing?" yelled Madinal. "They just injected the human! They just got the injection in one of their faces!"

"Shut up, Madinal. Not now!" shouted Sivas. "Go away! You've just shot my friend."

Madinal flew off. She couldn't believe Sivas's reaction.

The remaining Lorkun fairies came forward, ensuring that Harper's second and third attempts with the needle were batted away, but The Kingdom fairies were still strong, and Harper managed to complete the first full face of injections on Sandra.

Sivas sat down on the floor of the stage with Ax. He moved Ax's head into his lap for support.

Maye had just zoomed in on the TV in the out-of-bounds room. She was staring. She was praying.

"Get better. Get better. Get better," she was saying under her breath.

A tear escaped from her eye and started to roll down her cheek.

"I need to go down there. I need to intervene," said Maye, but she stood completely still, frozen, her eyes stuck on the screen.

Sivas put his hand on Ax's head then moved it gently into his hair.

Ax's eyes were closed.

His chest moved up and down slowly but steadily.

Maye stared at the rise and fall, praying, willing it to continue.

The movement in Ax's chest slowed down. It moved down, then up, then down, then it did not move back up.

Maye stared. She wiped a tear from her eye. She prayed again. "Up. Move up."

His chest moved suddenly and quickly up then down then stopped.

Maye stared.

Sivas removed his hand from Ax's head, moved out from underneath his body, and slowly lay Ax down on the ground.

"No," said Maye. "No."

Sivas took his shirt off and slowly, he placed it over Ax's chest, then pulled the top of the cloth over Ax's face.

Maye's eyes closed, and her head went down.

"Ahh......ahhhhhhhHHHHHHHHHHHHH" she screamed into her hands.

Her head came up as her cry became louder from deep in the centre of her being. The noise came out with the pain until the sound pierced through every molecule of energy and matter in The Kingdom, rippling through the mud and vibrating through every atom of the atmosphere, and down into Earth.

The fairies from The Kingdom stopped.

They could feel the pain coming from The Kingdom through everything that was vibrating on Earth. Maye's cry, a mother's cry, and they all knew what had happened.

They knew Ax was gone.

Maye let out one more cry of pain and turned to the Elders.

"Give me my bow," she said. "My baby, my baby, my baby."

Elson passed it to her. She swooped down to The Kingdom door. She flew in milliseconds through the fairy atmosphere. She arrived at the warehouse and immediately began to shoot arrows. The Elders were behind her, also firing arrows at every Lorkun fairy on the stage. They kept going and going and going until every last Lorkun fairy was either dead or gone.

Maye swooped down to where Ax was, terrified of looking at him. Terrified of touching his body in case it was empty.

Sivas had moved out of the way when Maye arrived. Maye knelt by Ax and pulled back the white cloth. She hesitated. She feared no longer being able to feel the spark of life in him. She placed her hands in his palms but felt only the texture of skin. He was gone. Maye placed her head on his stomach.

"My baby," she said through sobs. "I love you." Tears were streaming down Maye's cheeks, falling onto Ax's body. Cries of pain were escaping from her stomach. "I am so sorry for what I have done." Fairies from The Kingdom looked on. "You are with my father now." She let out another sob. She took a deep breath. She lowered her head and whispered, "The war has been won."

The tears continued to fall.

End of Part One.

For information about the release of **Part Two**, follow The Fairy Tale Fiction on Instagram and Twitter.

Printed in Great Britain
by Amazon

54096040R00180